The Wolf Effect

by

Mark W. Lyon

Copyright

Published by Mark W. Lyon
2972 Vale Court, Lake Oswego, OR 97034-7563 U.S.A.
www.markwlyon.us

Dedication

Dark Pueblo eyes,
Thick brown thighs

Prologue

~

The Wolf peered over the canyon rim down at the injured teenage girl. She lay trapped in a piñon pine on the face of the cliff below. Her body gripped by sharp stubby branches. Oddly contorted.

He saw a tear-streaked face. Smelled blood. Her eyes searched for help. They saw him and grew wide. He smelled fear. The scent floated up on the soft wind rising from Frijoles Canyon.

The moving air ruffled his grey coat. It brought a faint odor of burnt piñon. Wraiths of ancient cook fires lingered between the narrow canyon walls of soft Bandelier Tuff. Ghost signs of the Ancestral Pueblo dispossessed by drought more than four hundred years ago.

While the Wolf stared down with impassive yellow eyes, the hair of his grey coat stood up as if attracted by a static charge. He didn't notice. The Wolf was preoccupied. Searching his ageless memory. Trying to recall whether he had helped her ancestors. Whether he could help her.

Friday

~

"C'mon, Turkey. Out of the way," the Los Alamos County Sheriff cursed the pickup dawdling along New Mexico State Route 4 in front of his cruiser. The driver was either ignorant or arrogant, equally guaranteed to fracture the lawmen's patience. The sheriff hit the lights and siren, pulled into the oncoming lane, and felt the car lurch through a downshift and accelerate. The pickup driver, sensing a rising commotion, slowed and turned a blank stare toward the passing cruiser. The sheriff drew abreast, turned his head toward the driver and lowered his reflective shades so the old man could see the icicles shoot from his eyes.

Tom Winston had just turned forty-three. He was never troubled by ambiguity. Born and raised in Los Alamos, he'd joined the sheriff's office after graduating from Michigan State with a Master of Science in Criminal Justice. He approached his work with intelligence and proportion. However, this morning, he was not happy with his mission, one of the drawbacks of his job: bringing bad news to friends he'd known his whole life.

He turned off the highway and sped across a parking lot to one of the modern, single-story buildings housing the Los Alamos National Laboratories. The car swung into an empty slot near the entrance and jerked to a stop. The Sheriff grabbed his cap and bolted from the car.

Inside the sterile foyer, Winston fretted impatiently, standing before a gray metal desk. The only item on the surface was a triangular prism of wood with hand-carved lettering, "US Army Uplink Center." The uniformed Army Sergeant seated behind the desk regarded him with interest if not urgency. Civilian police rarely visited. Winston showed ID. The soldier retrieved a ledger from a drawer and dutifully recorded the arrival.

Winston bent forward, grabbed the offered pen and quickly scribbled in the log. A uniformed sentry left his position beside the American and California State flags to escort Winston to his destination. *Lest anyone forget the lab is part of the University of California,* he thought as he followed the sentry past the display.

~

The heart of the Uplink Center was the darkened Situation Room where soldiers evaluated high-resolution satellite imagery on monitors placed on every wall and desk.

Hayden Carlysle, still dressed like the bronc rider he had been twenty years ago, picked his way through banks of equipment to join his boss, Parker Davis, who was an engineer in his late forties. Parker had traded his pocket protector for a corner office four years ago. Among his other tasks, he now supervised the NANCY project, a proposal to identify innocent bystanders during urban warfare so the Army could avoid injuring them. Using software to analyze moving patterns in satellite imagery was Hayden's brain child and he was NANCY's chief scientist.

Hayden nudged Parker's shoulder to let him know he'd arrived. They stood behind a metal chair where US Army Major Elliot Grey sat glued to a monitor. The major was a Southerner, new to Los Alamos. He was watching a formation of US troops advance through a village and growing more agitated every minute.

Hayden watched Major Grey touch the screen where enemy figures had moved to an advantageous position against the US troops. "Damn yahoos," he drawled. "Delta's gonna get whupped like a rented mule. Where's tactical air?"

Hayden reached toward the screen and pointed to human figures near a building. "What about those civilians?"

"Noncombatants. Shouldn't be there," Grey scoffed.

"Let's ask NANCY for an evaluation," Parker suggested.

The major looked back over his shoulder. "I know she's supposed to be ready for deployment on Monday, Parker. But this—" he pointed to the monitor. "This is real. I can't risk it."

"Major—" Hayden began.

The major cut him off, "We don't want her lifting her skirts on us."

"C'mon, major," said Parker. "How will you ever know?"

The major considered for a moment, then snorted. "Okay. We'll give her exactly two minutes."

The three men watched the moving images, the enemy force, surround the US troops in under a minute.

Major Grey lost patience. "That's it!" He grabbed a phone beside the screen, punched a number and drawled harsh words into the mouthpiece.

Behind him, Hayden and Parker exchanged worried glances. Suddenly, flashes of bright light filled the monitor screen.

Hayden threw his hands in the air and spun in a circle. "Jesus, what the hell did you do?" He looked at Parker, appalled, and saw stunned disbelief on his boss' face. "So much for innocent bystanders," Hayden said with more sarcasm than he intended.

The major looked up at Hayden. "Hell's bells, you know what? Fifty percent of our munitions land on target in Afghanistan. That's three times better than the Gulf War." Grey ticked off on his fingers. "Precision munitions, unmanned drones, satellite targeting—we've done more than any nation in history to keep the innocent from harm."

"No argument there, major," Hayden said. "But damn, killing innocents is unacceptable. NANCY can prevent tactical commanders from inflicting unnecessary death. That's the whole point!" It was proving to be a tough sell.

The major stood and faced Hayden. "This is asymmetrical warfare, Carlysle. We've got belligerents in urban settings. We can't always discriminate between combatants and non-combatants. It doesn't work. If noncombatants die, our adversary is to blame, not us."

Hayden looked shocked. "That's your opinion. It's not Army policy."

"Indeed, Carlsyle. It is my opinion."

"Major, NANCY operates under the Law of War. You know, people have a fundamental right not to be harmed by others without their consent."

"Yes, and we believe that death or injury of innocents is always wrong, but, you will recall, the Principle of Double Effect: accidents can be excused if they were not the intended result of an act of war."

"The Principle of Double Effect is an excuse to tolerate collateral damage. NANCY will intentionally reduce it as far as possible. Our goal is for her to make ethical decisions on the battlefield better than human soldiers do."

The major shook his head, dismayed. "You have strict ethics, Carlysle. I admire how you've programmed them into NANCY, but this is war. Can't take the heat, don't start the fight. Collateral damage is as old as history and I, for one, don't see how in the Sam Hill NANCY can change that."

"Technology can help the Army adopt new ways, major," Parker added.

The major answered in a level tone. "Sir, I agree. But y'all have only 'til the end of next week to get it together. The Surge begins Monday and the Brass want this in place and ready for deployment. If you expect us to reauthorize your funding—"

The sudden appearance of a sentry and Sheriff Winston caused the major to stop mid sentence. He glared at the sentry, who had no trouble interpreting the major's hostile expression.

"He's cleared, sir," the sentry nodded at the sheriff.

Winston stepped closer to Hayden. "Hayden, I'm sorry to interrupt—"

"Sheriff," interjected Parker. "What's up?"

Winston ignored Parker, placed a friendly hand on Hayden's shoulder. "You gotta come. Your daughter took a fall."

Hayden looked puzzled as his mind switched gears. "What, Suzanne?"

"She fell," repeated the sheriff. "Frijoles Canyon."

"She all right?"

Winston offered his most compassionate expression. "They don't know."

Hayden started for the exit. "I gotta go."

Winston had to move quickly to catch up. "It's ten minutes. My car's outside."

"So's mine."

~

Hayden had been a rock jock all his life. He had no difficulty ascending the vertical face on the east side of Frijoles Canyon. The park rangers discouraged climbing in the remote canyon but he'd taught Suzanne and her twin brother, Keith, to scramble its various pitches during the early hours, before anyone took note. Now fourteen, the twins had been rock rats since they could walk.

He paused on the face to orient himself, find his route. He was aiming for a piñon pine where the park ranger had told him his injured daughter was trapped. He calculated that he'd arrived here in less than thirty minutes since Winston had received the reported. As Hayden reached for the next hand hold, he heard stones rattle around him. He glanced up, saw they came from the base of the piñon holding Suzanne. He shouted to the park ranger below on the talus slope, "Is the net here yet?" Hayden didn't wait for a reply, but continued rapidly up the face. After a few moments, he heard the ranger's voice drift up through the still air, "It's on the way. They're still having trouble getting by an accident on State Route 4."

Hayden was now ten feet below the piñon, growing more anxious because he still couldn't see his daughter. In a controlled voice he said, "Suzie, I'm here."

Her response, a sobbing painful moan, broke his heart. Hayden's desperation unleashed a surge of panic and he had to force himself to climb methodically. He ascended the last ten feet, and she was just within reach of his left hand.

When he finally examined her, Hayden felt a cold knife stab into his gut. Her body draped over the scrubby branches like a rag doll. Her bruised face stared into the sky. A broken tree limb protruded from a thick layer of red oozing from her right side. A trail of dried blood ran down the piñon bark below and spattered on the rocks. *My God, she's been pinned here for a long time.*

Hayden reached his hand to her face. His fingers brushed gently, avoiding the cuts and the large red bruise. "Oh, my poor girl. What did you do?"

Her mouth opened and closed like a fish. "I can't—" She squeezed her eyes to shut out the pain. *I've got to keep her conscious,* he thought.

"Okay, Suzie. We're going to get you down now. Do your best to relax."

"Wait—" she started to say, but the tree bucked ominously under her weight, the rupture sending a shower of rocks down the face. Alarmed, her head snapped toward him. Her eyes flared white.

Hayden's right hand groped for a secure hold. The tree shuddered again, sending more stones rattling down the cliff. She knew her peril. "Daddy!" He heard the panic.

His right hand found a hold. His left stretched for Suzanne. The tree gave way.

Hayden seized her right arm. He had her. He was holding. Squeezing tighter. Tighter. Clamped around the bones in her forearm. He gritted his teeth. Felt the knobby end of her wrist sliding through his grasp. He clenched tighter, determined to stop the slipping. He cried out when the bulge at the base of her thumb passed through his grip and clenched tighter. The carpal bones in her hand lingered in his hold just long enough to give him hope. Then, they wrenched free and she was gone.

Every sense etched an indelible record of that moment: her terrified eyes, her mouth open, the soundless scream, the rocks below. The child he loved tore from his hand, from his heart and fell away. He refused to believe his eyes. Still, she fell, caught in the piñon, caroming off rocks and trees. It took an eternity for the tiny bundle to smash onto the canyon floor but an instant for the sight of her broken, twisted body to shatter his heart.

~

Sheriff Winston watched Suzanne crash onto the talus, bounce once, and collapse in an awkward heap. Motionless. Only the piñon branches quavered around her body. He crawled toward her over the loose rock. The park ranger and young Tito Montoya scrambled after him. Maybe they could still do something, though he doubted it. The paramedics were still delayed by the accident on State Route 4.

She lay face up. Winston knelt beside her and put two fingers on her carotid artery. No pulse. A tree branch had torn a ragged hole in her abdomen. Blood stained her T-shirt and jeans. Her face had deep scratches. He turned her head to examine the large reddish-yellow bruise on her left cheek. The others hung their heads in mute understanding.

Suddenly, the sound of falling rock caused the men's heads to snap up, eyes to the cliff, fearing another tree was hurtling toward them. Instead, they saw Hayden sprawling, skidding,, plummeting out of control. He landed hard but bounced immediately to his feet and rushed over the rocks to Suzanne.

He fell to his knees beside his daughter, clasped her head in his bleeding hands, pressed her into his chest and rocked back and forth. The other men stood silent, listened to Hayden sob. Only young Tito moved. Winston watched him retreat down the trail toward the ranger station without saying a word to anyone..

~

What will I tell Lucy? Hayden braked to a stop in his driveway. The burden of carrying the news of Suzanne to his wife and son doused his last ember of spirit. He opened the driver's door of the Audi station wagon. Stepped out. Stood mindless and haggard, peering over the car at his well-kept suburban home on a mesa overlooking Los Alamos. The wind chilled his back. Billowing cumulus threatened the midday sun. The scrape of a wicker chair on wood drew his eyes to the front porch. His son, Keith, rose to his feet. Hayden called to him in a hollow voice. "Keith!"

The boy must not have heard because he vaulted over the porch railing. "Keith!" Hayden called louder, but his son dashed across the wind-blown yard and disappeared around the far side of the house.

Hayden gave the car door a listless shove. He trudged over to the porch, up the wooden steps to the screen door. He reached for the handle and stopped. He still didn't know how to tell Lucy. His left hand clenched the sash. He leaned his head on the wrist. The screen opened unexpectedly and startled him. He looked at his wife, her dark Pueblo Indian eyes glistening with welcome.

"I thought I heard your car." When she saw his distress, the smile vanished. "Oh, honey. What's the matter?"

He didn't want to look at her so he fixed his eyes on a point above her head in the empty room through the doorway. Without words, he put an arm around her shoulders and guided them into their home.

Inside the kitchen, a warm room, full of life, rich with color and texture, Hayden looked out of place, leaning back against the counter, staring into space.

Lucy listened to her husband then put one hand on the kitchen table to steady her rubbery legs. She let go, fell back into a chair. Her head nodded absently, her face slackened in denial, hoping for something, a reprieve.

Hayden stepped beside her, took her head in his arms, caressed her thick hair. Immediately thought of holding Suzanne while she grew cold on the talus. Now, he and his wife stared out the curtains at the emptiness beyond the kitchen window. After a long time she asked, "Does Keith know?"

"I will tell him."

Lucy waved a hand around in space. "He's around."

"Outside. I saw him."

Lucy's body heaved. She started to retch, pulled away from Hayden, and ran to the sink. When she finished spewing into the porcelain, she ran water, rinsed her mouth, and wiped her face before turning to Hayden.

"You saw her?"

"Yes."

"Alive?"

Hayden nodded, yes.

"Pain?"

He nodded more slowly, yes.

Lucy dropped her face into her hands. "My poor girl. What did she do?" She moved closer to Hayden, hugged him, and laid her head on his chest.

Hayden didn't know how long they stood together in the kitchen. When he felt that Lucy had calmed as much as she could, he headed upstairs to find Keith. As he approached the door to his son's room, it opened abruptly and the boy appeared in the hallway. His face was red and sad. He stopped when he saw his father.

Hayden stepped forward, held his arms out in an offered embrace, but Keith ducked under them and scooted down the hallway. Hayden half-turned and saw Keith stop at the edge of the stairwell and look down like he couldn't make up his mind about something. He looked back at Hayden for a moment, his expression filled with anguish, and then he was gone, down the stairs.

Hayden was puzzled, but relieved. He didn't have to describe the horrible tragedy again; endure his own guilt and devastation, or acknowledge that life as he knew it had ended that morning and he was now stumbling over obscure terrain to a place of unending despair.

Sunday

~

Hayden slept nearly two days. Lucy finally rousted him and insisted he dress for the wake. People were going to be arriving soon. He'd dressed, had coffee. Now he sat in his backyard, a dozen feet from the kitchen door, on a picnic table among trays prepared with food and drink. His mourning clothes showed dark and lustrous in sunlight. In his right hand he wielded a long-bladed hunting knife and took wicked hacks at the stick in his left hand.

He didn't notice Major Gray appear from around the side of the house, wearing his dress blues and carrying a large vase of white lilies, until the soldier greeted him. "Carlysle. Thought I'd find you here."

In spite of their disagreements, Hayden liked the major and was glad to see he'd shown up. "Major. Thanks for coming."

"Just wanted to convey my sympathy for your daughter."

The major's Southern charm always raised Hayden's spirits. "Thank you. Beautiful flowers."

"Did the sheriff say what happened?" Grey asked.

Hayden dropped his gaze, shook his head.

"I heard there was a young boy there who ran off?"

Hayden gave the major a questioning look.

"Small town. Lots of gossip," answered Grey.

"Yeah, I saw him." Hayden paused. "Who knows?"

"By the way, General Tolen asked me to convey his sympathy for your daughter," Grey said. Hayden nodded. "He fully understands your difficult and emotional situation and said he hopes that will not cause any undue difficulty with Friday's deadline."

Hayden gave a helpless shrug. "Well, that's just great."

"It's the Surge, Carlysle. They're going to deploy lots of troops. They believe your program will save civilian lives. Help win hearts and minds. Besides, it looks bad if the general misses the deadline."

Hayden looked down and hacked at the stick.

Major Grey pointed to the knife in Hayden's hand, "You got the right idea, Carlysle." The man's rolling drawl forced Hayden ever closer to a smile. "Where I come from, a man does your daughter wrong, you cut off his balls, roll 'em in corn meal, and fry 'em in bacon grease. Good for lunch with a tall bourbon and branch water."

Hayden nodded once to show the major his appreciation and a second time to direct him toward the house. "Lucy's inside. I'll be there in a minute."

Grey pivoted for the kitchen door. "Thank you. I will pay my respects to your wife."

Hayden's gaze followed Grey into the house. His knife-hand resumed its hack on the stick. The hint of a smile died on his lips. Through the kitchen windows, he saw Lucy talking with her parents. The knife seemed to hew its own steady rhythm. He saw Keith enter the kitchen, shoulders hunched forward as if he bore the entire burden of his sister's death.

The chopping continued and Hayden's picture of the kitchen receded in his mind's eye. Instead, he was looking down again into his daughter's eyes, felt his hand clutch her wrist, strain to keep her aloft. He saw his fingers turn white, her skin recede pore-by-pore through his faltering grasp. His beloved was falling again from his outstretched hand.

He blinked and shook his head. His left arm came back into focus, extended before him. He saw his left hand from the same perspective as in the vision. The hand opened. The stick dropped. He glared at his empty palm. Then he slashed it with the knife.

Sharp pain blurred his sense of time..Suddenly, he was sitting on the edge of the table, clasping a blood-soaked napkin around his left hand. Red drops fell onto the bench, speckled his boots.

He heard the kitchen door open and Parker's voice. "There you are. Lucy sent me to get you." Parker stopped when he saw Hayden's pale face and bloody hand. "My God, man. What happened?"

Hayden collected himself. "Parker. Oh. Nothing. I was carving. The knife slipped."

Parker's concern was sincere. "That looks serious. Let me see it."

"I'm okay."

Parker stepped quickly to Hayden and laid an arm around his shoulders. "Let's take care of this." He coaxed him from the table and Hayden lifted his clasped hands in the direction of the door into the garage.

"Thank you, Parker. I've got first aid in there."

Parker marched them to the garage. "Everything under control, Hayden?"

"I'm fine, thanks."

After they had treated Hayden's hand and wrapped it in gauze, Parker led them into the kitchen where acquaintances had gathered to grieve Suzanne. Hayden acknowledged each guest they passed with a nod or a handshake, sometimes a few words. He felt Parker touch his shoulder. "This business may affect our deadline, Hayden."

Hayden looked at his boss.

"What is this? First Major Grey and now you."

"Yeah, I heard what the general said. But we've got to keep pushing."

"Then what do you mean?"

"I expect those bad boys from ADSS will pay us a visit."

Hayden paused, confused. "Suzanne's accident had nothing to do with work."

"I know." Parker empathized with his chief scientist. "It's just that unexplained death disturbs their sense of security."

Hayden grew angry. "Well, then it can't go unexplained. We've only got four days

Lucy turned when she heard Hayden's voice, reached for his arm, and drew him into the circle with her parents and son. Lucy's father was eulogizing Suzanne. "In her voice I heard the thrush. In her face I saw the sunrise."

Lucy noticed Hayden's bandage. "Hayden, what happened to your hand?"

"I was careless with a knife. Parker here fixed it right up. We're fine."

"Some guys'll do anything for a day off," Parker joked and the circle opened to make room for him. Grandfather studied the bandage, then regarded Parker. "Good job, friend."

A moving body caught Hayden's attention and he saw Manny Montoya, Tito's father, who was also a family friend, and colleague—he worked as a construction supervisor for the lab—come through the door from the hallway that led to the front of the house. Lucy followed his look and when she saw Manny, she turned to greet him. Manny walked straight to Lucy and gently took her hands. "Lucy, I'm deeply sorry."

"Oh, Manny." She pulled her hands from his and threw her arms around his neck. "My dear man. I know you are. You've always been so kind to the children."

"I don't know how to express my—"

"I know," she interrupted. "Don't worry. I know."

Another body in motion drew Hayden's eyes away from Manny and his wife. He saw Keith disappear into the hallway.

~

Keith didn't think he could stand any more talk of Suzanne. He ached for his sister and nothing anyone said made him feel better. In the hallway, he jammed both hands into the front pockets of his jeans and headed for the front door. He passed Sheriff Winston talking with several men in the living room. Major Grey, who stood apart from the group, recognized Keith and extended his hand. "Hello, son."

Keith knew he'd been tagged. His right hand came out of his pocket and accepted the major's. "Hello, sir."

"I'm real sorry to about your sister," Grey said.

"Thank you, sir."

"You doing okay?"

"I guess so."

The major held his eyes. "Taking good care of your folks?"

Keith felt honored.

"You know, they really need all of your strength at a time like this."

Keith had never considered this. The major continued, tipping his head at Keith's pocketed left hand. "Whatcha got there?"

Keith withdrew the hand, opened it and revealed an intricately carved wolf fetish.

"Well, doggone!" Grey was truly surprised. He reached into his own pocket and produced one almost like it. "Identical, see?"

Keith scanned the major's trinket with skepticism. "No. They're carved by hand. Each one's different. Here. Mine has two black lines on the rim. Yours has one."

Grey had been surprised twice. He reexamined both icons. "Well, darn, son. If you ain't right."

Winston had been standing close enough to overhear the conversation and leaned between the two to confirm what Keith had said. He nodded agreement and then rejoined the other conversation.

Major Grey pocketed his trinket and gestured toward the kitchen. "Listen, son, good to see you, but I gotta go. Need to say good-by to your folks. You be sure to take good care of them now, ya hear?"

Keith was relieved. He watched the major head down the hall into the kitchen then he turned again toward the front door. As he reached for the handle, the door popped open and surprised him. Tito Montoya, Manny's son, charged in with a defiant look worthy of a Latin dictator. He strode right past Keith without seeing him and smack into the sheriff.

Winston placed a firm hand on Tito's forearm. Tito glared at Winston's hand then up into the tall man's face. "I want to pay my respects."

"We need to talk," the sheriff said in a nonthreatening voice.

"Then I'll come with you when I finish."

"No running?"

"I swear."

Winston let his hand drop. Tito twisted away and came face to face with Keith.

"Sorry about your sister, bro," Tito looked contrite.

Keith let himself go with it. "It's a killer, man."

"No lie there," Tito acknowledged. He backed away, turned for the kitchen.

~

Hayden watched Tito enter the room and approach Lucy. She embraced him. They held each other in shared sadness for a long time. Tito and the twins had been close friends since they started school together.

Later that evening, after the mourners had left, Hayden and Lucy settled in the kitchen. Hayden studied the half empty coffee cup on the table before him. Lucy shifted tableware and cooking utensils back and forth on the counter with no apparent plan. "I'm taking Keith to Grandma's tomorrow," she said.

"The boy's taking this hard," he said, then remembered. "Have him take that case of jars your folks forgot."

"I'll tell him."

"Parker says the lab's worried about security. They might keep me from finishing NANCY by Friday."

Lucy's hands dropped and she turned slowly revealing a face sodden with disbelief. "Are they out of their minds? Don't they know how many lives it will save? What it will mean for the Army? For the lab?"

He shared her sentiment but wanted to diffuse her anger. "It's just their way."

His wife fidgeted with her hands, then gave up, stuffed them into her armpits, and scowled. "Don't they have feelings?"

Hayden sighed. "Do they go with the job?"

Her exasperation festered even after they'd gone to bed. Hayden lay on his side facing the wall. Lucy sat beside him combing her hair with furious intensity.

"This security business. Isn't there anything you can do?" she asked.

"Sure. I need to find out what happened." He didn't move.

"What do you mean? You don't believe that she fell?"

"She fell. I did everything I could to save her, but I failed. That was my fault. How she wound up on that cliff in that tree, I don't know. I do know that she fell onto it." He gave a slight head shake.

"She was climbing?"

"Climbing or descending."

Lucy shook her head, perplexed. She put the hairbrush on the bedside table and lay beside Hayden. He felt her warm hands on his shoulders, inhaled the vanilla scent of hand cream.

"You did everything you could, Hayden. Don't blame yourself."

"I can't help it. I feel like I should have done more."

"What more should you have done?"

"I should have saved her!"

"Oh Hayden. It wasn't your fault." Lucy paused then changed direction. "Well, what do you think happened before you arrived?"

"I saw a bruise on her face," he said. "It had antiseptic. Someone or something had hit her earlier."

Lucy continued to caress his shoulders in silence.

"Your daughter was getting to that age, Hayden."

"What do you mean?"

"Nothing specific. It's just that, lately, I felt like she wasn't telling us everything."

"Someone was with her."

"How do you know that?"

Hayden rolled to face his wife. "I design systems that can distinguish patterns between innocent behavior and people with hostile intent. My sense is that Suzanne would not have fallen on her own. There must have been something else."

"If someone was with her," she rose on her elbow. "Does that mean you think it wasn't an accident?"

He laid on his back, looked at the ceiling. "I don't know, but I'm desperate to find out—for our peace of mind and because I can't finish NANCY until this thing is resolved. I'm going to find Sheriff Winston in the morning. See what he knows."

Lucy let her head fall onto the pillow beside him, reached out and squeezed his shoulder. "Action has always been one of your sterling qualities."

He reached an arm around her waist and pulled them closer. "And loving wife has always been one of yours."

Monday

~

The next morning, Keith entered the Los Alamos Country Sheriff's Office. The uniformed duty sergeant seated behind the reception desk held a coffee cup in one hand and a phone in the other. He glanced up with an expression that said he hoped this arrival wasn't trouble, then muffled the phone on his chest, and shot Keith a questioning look.

"Hi. Can I see Tito Montoya?"

The sergeant gestured to an open doorway. Keith acknowledged with a nod and walked through a door with an eye-level plaque that read, "Jail Intake." He spotted Tito sitting on a bunk staring at the wall in one of the four cells. The other three were empty. All of the cell doors were ajar. He stepped into Tito's cage, but his friend didn't look at him.

"Why are you still here?" Keith asked.

Tito kept staring. "Nowhere else to go."

"Got something for you." Keith pulled the wolf icon from his pocket and flipped it toward him. Tito saw it in time to snatch it from the air. When he recognized it, he smiled and looked at Keith.

"Thanks, man. Where'd you find it?"

Keith squinted hard at Tito. "On Burnt Mesa."

Tito lowered his eyes. He looked down at the icon for a long time before he spoke in a quiet voice. "I did something bad, bro. You ain't gonna like it."

~

Hayden arrived at the Sheriff's Office a few minutes after Keith. He approached the desk sergeant, still on the phone, and got the same questioning look.

"Morning. Sheriff in?"

The Sergeant nodded to an open office and waved for Hayden to enter. Inside the small room, he found Winston leaning back in the chair behind his desk reading a report. The Sheriff acknowledged Hayden with a smile. When Hayden drew up a chair and lay his injured hand on the desk, Winston leaned forward and examined the bandage.

"You forget your scout training?"

"I was preoccupied."

Winston shook his head and reprimanded him, "Pay attention, will you?"

Hayden retrieved his hand, embarrassed, nodded. Then asked, "So?"

"I wish I could tell you something but, at this point, we don't know much."

Hayden leaned forward with a look of anticipation.

"I talked to Tito," Winston continued. "He and Suzanne went to Burnt Mesa together."

"They did?" Hayden's eyes widened with surprise.

"Seems they were biking around the loop through White Rock and decided to stop and enjoy the view."

Hayden groaned.

"They got in an argument," Winston said.

"Did he say what about?"

"Yeah, high school stuff. One of the teachers was playing favorites with Suzanne. Tito doesn't like that teacher. They got into an argument and he left."

"But she was okay?"

"Tito's got a short fuse, like his father. He said he left because he didn't want to lose it."

"You believe him?"

"Yeah. I do."

"She had a bruise on her face. Someone had treated it earlier."

"Yeah, I saw it."

"You don't think Tito could have hit her?"

"It's possible that he didn't tell me everything. But, do I think he pushed Suzanne off a cliff? No."

"So, we know why she was there, but not how she fell."

"That's about it."

"Well something sure as hell happened up there and the uncertainty is eating me alive."

Winston folded his hands on the desktop and looked at Hayden with an expression that said he'd been here before. "A tragedy like this is terrible. It tears some families apart. Others stay together. They're the ones who worked very hard—and I mean very hard. It's what you've got to do, Hayden"

"It was my daughter, Tom. I feel responsible. I need to know what happened."

The sheriff looked at his friend with a comforting smile. "Her death was not your fault, Hayden. At this point, the most likely scenario is that she accidentally fell from the cliff. We have no reason to believe otherwise. But if it does turn out to be something different, we'll find out and I'll let you know. "

Hayden contemplated the sheriff's words.

"Listen, I know your world is abstract," he teased.

Hayden smiled.

"Always has been. Now I hear you're working to save the innocents of the world with a computer program. Tell me, professor, how's a computer gonna protect anyone?"

Hayden didn't appear to have a handy response. Winston continued. "Hayden. Right now, you need to be here. Not in your head. Your family needs you rock-solid. I swear, as soon as we learn something I'll let you know."

~

In the Jail Intake, Keith crossed the cell and sat on the thin mattress next to Tito, who gave him a glum look. "What it is, bro."

He listened to Tito's story, eyes focused on the bars of the cell, watching it unfold in his mind like a movie.

"Friday morning, me and Suzanne biked the loop around White Rock. We got to Bandelier and she wanted to check out the sunrise, so we stopped. We're sitting on Burnt Mesa just holding each other, keeping warm. I looked over and she flashed me that teasing look of hers and hit me with one of those stupid questions she was always asking: 'Do you think a girl should be a virgin?'"

"She said that?" Keith was mildly surprised.

"You know how she was," Tito shrugged. "I told her it didn't really matter to me. So right there she starts taking off her clothes." He looked at Keith. "I swear to God, man, It's the truth."

Keith searched Tito's face, "Your shitting me."

"No man, I'm telling you. She turned into this, like, crazy woman. She was all over me. I didn't know what to do. I just went with it."

"What do you mean, 'You went with it?'"

"It just happened, man. Shit, it's so fucking hard to tell you this. I mean like, what could I do? Here's this beautiful naked girl, we've known each other forever and—I mean, I thought about her being your sister, but, she was, like, always my friend, too and then—yeah, I couldn't help myself, but I guess I thought, somehow it would be okay."

"Fuck!" Keith watched Tito's expression transform into a pathetic, pleading smile. Waves of emotion flooded over him. In confusion, he looked down at his shoes. He struggled to listen to Tito. "Afterwards, she says, 'You were a virgin, right?' And I was like, 'Me? What are you saying?' Then she snuggled up like it was okay."

Keith's head was in his hands and he could barely hear Tito over the outrage in his head.

"When I asked her how would she know," Tito said. "She got, like, all uppity and stuff and said she had been with older guys. So I was like, 'Oh yeah? Name one.' I thought it was bullshit. She told me that I wouldn't want to know. I told her she was a lying sack of shit and she said she wasn't. So I dared her to tell me. She was like, 'What if it was someone you know?'" He looked again at Keith.

"She was pissing me off, so I told her to go fuck herself. "

Keith looked up at Tito and waited.

"You know what she said? Manny! She said she fucked my old man."

"I don't believe it," Keith was stupefied.

Tito's eyes grew larger. "Yeah, she got right in my face, man. Said he gave her a ride home last summer and she made him fuck her in the front seat of his truck."

"And you believed her?" Keith looked at Tito in disbelief.

"Man, I didn't know what to think. But it's like she was trying to piss me off or something. I threw that wolf icon at her. Then she laughed and stood up. I stood up, too. She got that fake surprised look on her face and said how cool it was that she fucked the father and the son. I went to grab her——"

"This is some fucking sick shit." Keith looked into Tito's eyes, saw again the pleading, pathetic look.

"I didn't want to hurt her," Tito said. "She started running fast toward the edge of the canyon, but you know I'm faster. I caught her right away, pulled her down from behind.

"She stood up. I thought she'd quit, but she kept laughing. She wouldn't stop, man. I couldn't help it. I just wanted her to shut up. I knocked her down.

"She got up and her face was all red on one side. She spit at me. Screamed 'Fuck you.' at me."

"Wait, you hit her?" Keith's voice took on an edge.

"I'm telling you, man. I totally lost it." He stopped and gave Keith a pleading look. "Then she got afraid. You know, her eyes got wide and she screamed like I never heard before."

~

In Winston's office, Hayden understood his friend's advice, but needed him to understand the scope of the problem. "The Army's got a deployment coming up and they have given us until Friday to finish our work."

"Okay."

"I need to make some refinements before then. But Suzanne's fall has security worried for some reason and I can't get access until they know for sure what happened to her."

"That's easy. I just tell them she fell."

"It's not that simple, Tom. This is Los Alamos. National Security? They look at every incident with a microscope so they can know, with 100 percent certainty, whether it has significance or not."

"Gimme a break," Winston looked to one side. "There is no connection between her fall and your work." He looked at Hayden "It's more important for you to keep this tragedy from taking your wife and son. They need you to be in control of yourself."

"No. You don't understand. This project—"

"Hayden! What's important? C'mon."

The office door opened and the sergeant poked his head through.

"Sorry to interrupt, sheriff. There's a couple out here. They're—" He glanced at Hayden then back to Winston. "I really need your help."

Winston stood, looked at Hayden. "Excuse me. I'll be right back."

He left Hayden sitting alone. In the quiet, he started to hear conversation through the walls, muffled but intelligible.

~

Tito turned his body so he faced Keith on the bed next to him. "I'm so fucking sorry, man. I totally blew it."

Keith fumed. "Fuck, Tito! She was my sister!"

"I know. I'm sorry." He hung his head.

"Fuck!"

Tito kneaded his hands.

Keith stood and loomed over him . "I saw her face. Jesus. What the fuck to do now?"

Tito stood. He looked guilty, but with a strong hint of defiance. "I swear I didn't want to hurt her."

Tears came to Keith's eyes. "She was my sister. She never hurt anyone."

Tito was frustrated. He lost his temper. "She was a fucking whore."

Keith threw a right fist at Tito's head. It slammed into his left ear. Tito stumbled, surprised, protected the ear with both hands and quickly recovered his balance. Keith saw the insolence that covered his pain.

"You don't know shit," Tito spat.

~

Through the walls, Hayden recognized Tito's voice. He stood up, his body tensed, and listened to the emotion hammering through the wall. "I was there. I heard her. She fucked everyone and she fucking-well deserved what she got."

Hayden flushed with anger. He kicked the chair and stormed out the office.

~

Keith faced Tito, his feet apart, fists balled, ready to swing. "She was not a tramp. She was my sister. And you fucked her up."

Tito glared. One hand rubbed his injured ear.

Keith let his hands drop. "Well, fuck you. I got my own problems." He turned and stomped out of the cell. As he was about to leave the intake room, he looked back at Tito, "All this time I thought you were our friend."

Tito slumped like an abandoned hound.

~

Hayden drove blind. Rage occluded his vision and all he could see in the pinpoint of light ahead was painted lines streaking toward him on the highway. Blackness lay to either side, above and below. He was not conscious of his foot jammed on the accelerator or his white fingers locked around the steering wheel. No thoughts. Empty mind. Only a pervasive fury that grew hotter and wrenched his body. When the tension finally peaked, he swung his right fist up and bashed the headliner. His hand felt nothing. He shouted the words that came through the jail wall, Tito's words: "I was there. I hurt her. She fucking-well deserved what she got."

In that moment, his guilt suddenly dissipated and he felt like he'd just set down a tremendous weight. *It wasn't me*, he thought. *She was pushed.* The blackness around the tunnel of his vision began to recede. He saw a turnoff. At the last minute, Hayden flung the wheel right. The blue Audi drifted around the corner, slid wide off of the pavement and bounced sideways through the sage on the far side of the road. His mind instantly snapped back to the present. Hayden controlled the station wagon, maneuvered back onto the pavement and then swerved to avoid an oncoming pickup. He flipped off the other driver and pressed his foot down on the accelerator. *Tito.* His mind grasped at the name like a drowning man at a life preserver.

~

Manny Montoya saw a blue station wagon careen around the corner in front of him and slide into the sagebrush. Instinctively, he took his foot off the gas and held his breath waiting for it to flip over. When it suddenly recovered and came straight at him, he was too shocked to react. Fortunately, the car veered past him at the last minute. He glimpsed the driver's hand give him the bird. Manny wasn't having a good day.

He tried not to think about the near miss as he sped to the Arroyo Bowl. When he reached the sputtering neon sign, he swung the pickup into the parking lot, onto a moat of bare dirt that circled a rectangular, cinderblock fort, the lone defender on this deserted crossroad. The pickup slalomed through the caliche, scattering a mantle of dust over the high mileage relics that were haphazardly abandoned by patrons in their eager quest for booze.

Manny aimed for an empty spot, but turned away when he saw four men fighting there. He recognized Sanrio Machuque wailing away on three other Indians. Manny took the next empty spot, parked, got out, and marched past the scuffle to the windowless building's only door. He pointedly ignored the fight, thinking to himself, *I beat the shit out of that arrogant* cabrón *in high school and he still doesn't get it.*

He let the steel door close behind him and strutted into the dark, low ceilinged sanctuary, past the tables and chairs built to withstand periodic flights across the room. He knew most of the patrons, but wasn't in the mood. However, he was amazed to see his wife, Rachael, at a table drinking with her girlfriend Jose, the one who was always bumping him with her big tits. *One of these days*, he told himself. The bruise on the side of Rachael's face had grown more visible since last night.

He stopped beside their table. "Rachael! What the fuck are you doing here?"

Both women looked up at the sound of the voice. When Rachael recognized Manny, her fingers jumped to her discolored cheek.

"Manny! You surprised me."

"I didn't see your car outside."

Rachael looked away. "No. It wouldn't start. Sanrio gave me a ride."

"Machuque? I just saw him outside." Manny leaned his hands on the table. "That horse turd still sniffing around? I told you to stop seeing that bag of shit."

Rachael impulsively rubbed her face.

"I'm gonna go get Tito from jail," Manny informed her.

Rachael looked a Jose. "Bout time."

Manny took a deep breath, grabbed a chair, spun it around, and straddled it with his back to the steel door. "I ran into Winston a while ago. He said something about Tito and that girl in Jémez Springs last year."

Rachel looked perturbed. "Nothing ever came of that."

"Winston's a jerk-off," Jose chimed in.

"You know how cops think," said Manny. "Where there's smoke, there's fire. I think Tito came to mind because he was in the canyon when Suzanne fell and she had a bruise on her face." He reached one hand toward Rachael and grinned. "Kinda like yours."

Rachael gave him a dirty look and turned to Jose. "Tito liked Suzanne," she said.

"Yeah," Manny flashed his white teeth. "She was a looker."

Rachael studied him briefly and shook her head. "You always did worship that Carlysle woman and her kids."

Manny's smile became a sneer. "Shove it, Rachael."

"That's right," Jose said to him. "I remember you and her in school."

"You too, Jose. Stuff it."

Jose ignored him. "Didn't you and them used to see each other at church all the time?"

"Jose! Shut the fuck up," he snapped.

"Let her alone, Manny. She's just saying what she saw."

Like I need more of this shit? Manny thought. He braced his hands on the table, ready to stand. At that moment, a streak of light lit up the room as Sanrio pushed open the steel door. He brushed the dust from his jeans and swaggered toward Rachael's table. The two women looked at him. He recognized Manny and stopped in his tracks.

The women exchanged a quick look, which piqued Manny's interest, and he glanced over his shoulder. At the sight of Sanrio, he scowled. The Indian turned quickly and detoured into the bowling alley.

"I gotta get Tito," Manny said and dismounted the chair. He didn't head for the steel door but headed into the bowling alley. He walked toward a table where Sanrio sat, facing away, beer in hand, talking to three men standing around the ball return.

Manny knew Sanrio didn't see him approaching from behind. The Indian kept talking, unaware, then stood, walked to the return and retrieved a ball. Manny stopped when he got to Sanrio's table. He gave a loud snort, clearing phlegm from his nose and the back of his throat, and hawked it into Sanrio's beer glass.

Sanrio heard the hack and saw the smirk on the faces of his friends. He turned just in time to see Manny spin on his heel and saunter for the exit. The Indian was enraged. He flung the ball in Manny's general direction.

Manny didn't turn around. He knew it would be a lame throw. *He'll never fight me.* He smiled to himself. Maybe not such a bad day.

~

Winston leaned against the desk in the reception area of the Sheriff's office. Manny and Tito stood before him. He set his coffee cup on the desk and picked up a handful of papers. Looking at Manny, he said. "The boy's free to leave. We weren't holding him. Just let him stay because he said he had nowhere to go."

Manny turn to Tito. "He has a home."

"Bullshit!" Tito's defiance went beyond teenage rebellion, Winston observed.

"Boy, you have a home, you know it so don't give me any shit," Manny's voice was firm.

Tito sneered. "What would you know about a home?" He turned away and shambled to the front door.

Winston watched him leave. "I worry about that boy, Manny. I hope I don't see him here again."

"Not if I can help it, Tom."

~

A cloudless afternoon is rare in the spring, Keith thought as he watched his mother drive through the pueblo. She brought the Subaru to a stop on the barren dirt in front of Grandma's small cinderblock house. Grandma refused to move away from her family dwelling to any of the newer and nicer homes. Lucy exited the driver's side, walked around the car and opened the passenger door. Keith stared at his feet and didn't move.

"Are you going to tell me why you got so upset this morning?" his mother asked.

"I already said. It's what happened with Suzanne. Can you quite bugging me about it?"

"All right, Keith. Please don't just sit there. Go find your cousin."

Keith surveyed the terrain through the windshield. "If he's even here. He's probably hunting."

"We'll be here a while," she said, trying to sound understanding.

"All right. I'll look."

"Come back when you're finished. Grandma will want to see you."

She left the door open and he listened to her footsteps retreat across the hard ground. Keith didn't really want to sit but he didn't feel like moving either. He swung his right leg onto the running board, leaned on the upraised knee. He looked again out the windshield and saw his cousin, Rafer, prancing toward him. *He must have heard the car*, thought Keith, and noticed the wrist rocket dangling from Rafer's right hand and the two rabbits from his left. *Lucky guy. Hunts whenever he wants.*

When Rafer reached the car he stopped beside the open door and leaned on the roof. He offered his condolences in Keres, their native tongue.

"Suzanne is peaceful, now."

Keith couldn't see Rafer's face above the door but he nodded and answered in Keres, "Yes. And my heart is cold."

"No wonder. A warm sister has left it." Rafer stepped away from the car, an invitation for Keith to stand. "Somoma said for you to come."

Keith looked up at Rafer and rose slowly out of the car. He liked the Shaman but hadn't seen him recently. The old man probably wanted to commiserate over Suzanne. He pictured the Shaman's artful house among the cottonwoods and smiled.

After the short walk, the boys came to the well-kept adobe home. A ladder slanted against the front porch. The lean Indian painting the cornice from the top rung didn't look eighty years old.

Rafer greeted him. "Shaman, I brought you someone."

Somoma saw Keith and jumped off the ladder. He dropped the paint brush on a pile of rags, rushed over and grabbed Keith. They embraced for a long time. Finally, Somoma said, "A very sad thing. We all loved your sister."

"Thank you," Keith said into the Shaman's ear. "It is hard to think of life without her."

Somoma released Keith and drew back to look at him. "I know. I wanted to see you. It is time to make the awakening. It may help you."

"Now?" Keith was unprepared.

"No. My son needs me today. He's moving a refrigerator. Thursday." The Shaman's expression told Keith the issue was settled. Somoma turned, strode to the pile of rags, retrieved the paint brush and climbed the ladder. Keith looked at Rafer. They both shrugged and left the old man to his work.

~

The two teenagers walked past Grandma's house to the Subaru. Keith hefted the crate of jars from the trunk and stashed them in the shed. Then he followed Rafer into the cozy living room of the house. They sprawled quietly on a sagging couch and waited for the women to finish their conversation. They also spoke Keres. From the sound of silverware clinking in the kitchen, they were eating at the table, the center of life in Grandma's home. Keith heard his grandmother ask, "What does your husband say about this accident?"

"He runs circles in his head. One minute, he's sad; the next, angry," his mother replied.

"How will you help him?"

"We don't know what happened," Lucy said. "The mystery feeds his anger. The anger clouds his reason. He seeks truth but craves revenge."

"Like all men," Grandma scoffed.

"I want to help him but my girl's death confounds me."

"It is your duty, child. To help him find the right path. The future of your family depends on you."

"I have so much sorrow." His mother's voice sounded far away.

"You have so much strength," Grandma replied.

"I feel so weak."

"Your spirit is now the rabbit to flee with the first sound? No! It must be the bear to stand and fight!" Keith had never heard anyone speak like that to his mother. He wasn't sure whether the sudden scrape of a chair on the wood floor meant that Grandma was angry or she knew they were waiting in the living room.

"Boys, come. Eat some cake," she shouted.

They didn't need a second invitation and ran into the kitchen. Keith gave the old woman a warm embrace.

"Grandma, I put some jars for you in the shed," he said. She smiled at him but he was watching Rafer grab a seat and reach for the cake. He had to move quickly to claim his share.

Grandma moved beside his mother and stroked her hair. "The signs are difficult for you now."

"I will study them harder, mother." Keith shoved a huge piece of chocolate cake in his mouth and marveled at the respect in his mother's voice.

~

Hayden bent over an industrial lathe he kept in his garage and machined an elaborate handle that would complete the angular metal box resting on the bench behind him. He sought distraction. He'd thought only of Suzanne since he had left the jail. Somehow the NANCY project hadn't entered his mind.

After a few passes with the cutting tool, Hayden unwound the cross-feed wheel, withdrew the tool from the work and straightened his back. With one hand, he flipped the switch to stop the headstock. With the other, he lifted his goggles to the top of his head and drew the shirt sleeve across his sweaty forehead. He glanced at a portrait of Suzanne over the bench and felt a surge of anger. He considered moving the picture to the back wall of the garage with the dozens of other photos of a happy family in search of fulfillment, but the garage had become troublesome with its catalogue of memories: the dusty tandem stroller, rubber boots with froggy faces and sunflowers, pink and blue snowsuits, a ninja skateboard, tasseled roller blades, twin bikes with training wheels, short skis, sleeping bags, a saddle, a hang glider, belaying ropes, a motorcycle helmet, fishing rods, folding camp chairs, a kiln, machine tools, an old pickup cloaked in canvas in the far bay.

Standing alone in the garage, he could not escape the sorrow of Suzanne's death. Or the anger toward Tito, *He was their friend. What happened? Did he push her? Over a simple argument? It must have been more. He called her a whore. She wouldn't have sex with him! Tito told Winston he didn't lose his temper and Winston believed him. Does the sheriff know what Tito screamed in his cell?*

At the sound of tires crunching over the gravel driveway, he turned and saw Lucy's Subaru pull up to the open garage door. She stepped out and leaned her arms over the car door like she couldn't wait to speak.

"Hayden! Sheriff Winston let Tito go."

Hayden was dumbfounded. He dropped his hands and stared. He saw her puzzled reaction. "What?" she asked.

"Strange, that's all." He advanced a couple of steps. "I heard him yelling. He said Suzanne deserved everything she got."

Lucy didn't understand. "Tito?" She moved around the car door and came toward him.

Hayden double-checked his memory. "He said he was there. He hurt her." *I have correctly identified an aggressor,* he told himself.

As she drew near, he saw her skepticism and unconsciously jammed both hands into his front pockets. "I swear I would kill anyone who hurt Suzanne."

Her harsh look stung him like a slap. She stopped within arm's reach. "You can't be serious."

"Are you taking his side?"

He felt her hands go to his shoulders. "I am not taking his side. I meant about--"

He cut her off. "It's that soft spot you have for Manny, isn't it?"

She stepped back. "What makes you bring that up after all these years?"

"Seeing you two together yesterday." He winced at the bleating sound of his own voice.

"You know that ended the day you asked me to marry you."

He turned his head aside. "He still carries a torch."

"Hayden, control yourself. Try to understand what's really happening."

"I do. There's a crime but no justice."

"Justice is Sheriff Winston's business. Ours is reconciliation."

Hayden didn't like it. "But he set Tito free."

She took both of his hands, shook them in the space between them to emphasis each statement. "Forget Tito. What about your project, your son, our future? Let's move past this, together." Then she dropped his hands, stepped forward and wrapped him in a deep hug.

Tuesday

~

The next morning, Hayden drove the Audi to Valle Grande, a serene 25,000-acre meadow that carpeted the Valles Caldera, the picturesque volcanic crater in the Jémez Mountains. Major Grey was waiting for him by the main gate on Highway 4. Hayden waved for him to get into the station wagon and the two men road the graveled trail past the visitor's center to the northwest side of the valley. Hayden stopped the Audi in a pullout next to Parker's pickup. He grabbed two day packs from the back of the car, gave one to the major and they hiked out into the lush grassland to meet Parker.

The air was still; the temperature, comfortable at a fast walk. The sun incandesced in a cloudless blue sky. They had covered considerable ground when the major suddenly realized the enormity of the meadowland.

"Carlysle, we walked and we walked and nothing's changed. What the hell is this place?"

Hayden chuckled. "Some years ago, about 1.4 million, a volcano blew here and left a crater about twelve miles wide. Three hundred thousand years later, it blew again and created these hills you see inside the bowl."

"You're saying it farted twice through the same hole?"

"You certainly have a way with words," Hayden's eyes slide sideways. "But yes, that is what happened."

"It is some piece of real estate. My idea of a prosperous, old-time cattle ranch."

"The valley has an interesting history and you're right, it was once part of the King Ranch. Now it's a land trust. The trustees are trying to make it profitable, but they're not doing as well as they hoped."

"People would pay for this view," Grey was awestruck.

"Yeah," Hayden allowed. "Some do. Not sure we need any more."

"Did I just hear the wing beats of passing elitism, Carlysle?"

Hayden smiled and kept walking. After a while, he spotted a white gyrfalcon circling in the blue dome overhead. He looked around for Parker but the valley's huge size deceived his vision, made it difficult to isolate and focus. Finally, the shape of man in camouflage clothing snapped into view from amid the landscape's green and brown hues.

Hayden tapped Grey on the shoulder and pointed up at the raptor. Just as the major saw it, the bird plummeted into the dry grass and rose with a prairie dog in its talons. It flew straight to Parker and landed on his gloved forearm.

Parker held up the rodent so Hayden and Grey could see it. Both men nodded approval and stepped toward him through knee-high brush. Parker hooded the bird and they all examined the catch.

"Well, that's number three, gentlemen," Parker said, looking flushed. "What did you say earlier, major? He wouldn't get one?"

"I have to admit, the bird is good, Davis. First time I've seen one in action."

"He's even better on waterfowl," Hayden added. "Come back in the fall. I promise you won't go hungry."

With one hand, Parker tucked the game into a pouch on the back of his jacket while he looked at the two men. "Glad you both made it," he said. "What say we give Merlin a rest and grab a bite ourselves." He gestured toward a stand of Ponderosa pine on a nearby hillside. "I got a favorite spot right over there. Hellava view."

They set off with Parker leading. When they arrived at the nose of the ridge that Parker had indicated, they saw before them the immense savanna that filled the entire crater like a pale green lake. They dropped their daypacks. Hayden rolled out a blanket and Grey helped him arrange lunch. Parker drove a metal perch into the soil for Merlin and dismembered one of the prairie dogs for the bird's meal.

Then they sprawled on the ground and dove into an early lunch.

"Major, I invited you here today to see this exquisite landscape," Parker said while he set a beer can in the grass. "Did Hayden tell you much about it?"

"Just enough to tickle my curiosity."

"This area is unique in human history," Parker said. "Twice, man discovered his most devastating instruments of war here." He pointed in the direction of Los Alamos. "Just over that hill, the atom bomb, seventy years ago." He turned to Grey with a sweep of hands that took in the entire valley. "In this caldera, the obsidian arrowhead, seventy centuries ago."

The major studied Parker and then seemed to shiver in the midmorning air. "A strange confluence, if I say so myself. No wonder it's called the Land of Enchantment."

"Not sure that's what the PR people had in mind, but I'll go with that," Parker said.

"Damned if it isn't enchanted," Grey continued. "Between the scenery and the food here, I could be happier than a dead pig in the sunshine."

Parker laughed. "We're glad you could join us, major." He glanced at Hayden. "Good for Hayden, too. Get out in the open. Clear the mind."

Grey lowered the chicken leg he was gnawing and looked at Hayden. "Anything further about that boy, Carlysle?"

Hayden turned to the major with a dark look. "The sheriff doesn't think so, but there's definitely something there. I'm working on it."

Grey saw that the topic was off limits and switched gears. "I didn't realize 'til yesterday that your wife is an Indian girl.".

Hayden's eyes were still on the major and he couldn't tell whether he heard social comment or a Southern drawl that shaded it that way. He let it go. "We were kids in school together."

"School's here integrated?" His tone bordered on incredulous.

Parker looked away, seemed to study something in the distance.

"Her dad worked for the lab," Hayden said. "They lived in Los Alamos. She grew up there. She's half Pueblo, but off the res, as they say. Got her PhD in Santa Fe."

"She is most certainly a fine woman."

Parker suddenly ducked his head and whispered. "Son of a gun! Nobody move!"

The men froze at the urgency in Parker's voice. After a moment, Hayden asked, "What?"

Parker pointed with his chin to a spot in the distance."Turn your heads real slow." The two men followed his gaze. "The edge of the field. By those pines," he said.

They scanned the brush for several moments where Parker had indicated and then Grey's face lit up in surprise. "That's a damn wolf, Parker."

Hayden saw it too and whispered, "It is a wolf. He's upwind."

They watched the animal prowl the tree line for a dozen yards and then disappear into the shadows.

"Never seen one this far south," Parker mused.

"I didn't know you had wolves in New Mexico," Grey said.

"Ranchers killed 'em off in the 1920s," Hayden said. "We have a program with Arizona to restock Mexican wolves—"

"But there's only about fifty," Parker interjected. "And they're all in the southwestern part of the state. Besides, they're a lot smaller than he was."

"I heard of only one other gray around here," Hayden said. "Up at Ted Turner's place on the Colorado border."

They looked at each other.

"Well, this is truly inspiring," Grey said after a minute had passed.

Hayden glanced at him. "My wife's family would say it's a sign."

"How's that?"

"Some Indians believe that wolves know a man's fate. When the wolves around here disappeared, they abandoned men, left their lives in chaos. Seeing a wolf now could signal a new order, life about to change."

"Sounds like a good sign," said the major.

"That depends on the essential nature of your spirit," Hayden replied.

Grey turned toward Hayden. "How do you know what that is?"

Hayden smiled at him. "Ask a wolf."

"On that thoughtful note, gentlemen," Parker said. "Merlin says it's time to head back." Parker rose to collect the gyrfalcon, who was busy studying the landscape with predatory intensity.

~

Sanrio Machuque's monster truck idled in Manny Montoya's gravel driveway. He sat in the elevated cab behind the wheel, surveyed the orderly yard in front of the adobe home below him, and smirked. "That *cabrón* thinks he has everything," he muttered. His gaze followed Rachael with considerable amusement as she tottered through the front door of the house in her high heels, turned her back toward him, taking the opportunity to show off her shapely rear while locking the door, and sashayed toward the truck with a wayward body motion that alternately strained the fabric of her jeans and separated the buttons of her blouse.

At this short distance, Sanrio saw that her makeup didn't hide the bruise on her face. He watched her attempt to climb into the cab in tight jeans and when she succeeded on the third try, he accepted her soft, prolonged kiss.

"Mm, I been dreaming about how good that was gonna feel," she said when she stopped to catch her breath.

"Yeah, Chica," he replied. "Close the door so we can scoot." She reached for the door and he shifted into reverse. The truck rumbled out of the driveway, jerked to a stop and then accelerated forward onto the pavement

Sanrio glanced sideways at Rachel. "You looking mighty good for going to work."

She was busy fumbling through her purse. "Machuque, you ain't heard nothing about them widening the highway by Grovenor's?"

He thought for a moment. "Nope. But if it was gonna happen, I'd know."

"Why? You got some Indian lore you hasn't told me about?"

He flashed a cocky smile. "Me and that guy, Freddy, in the state office, we're tight."

Rachael guffawed. "He's your buddy now? I thought you kicked the shit out of him."

Sanrio twisted his head back and forth and mumbled, "Fucking women. Never understand." He turned to her. "That's how men bond. *Somos hermanos*!"

She looked dubious. "Yeah? When are you and Manny gonna bond?"

"Shit, that weak *maricón*. He will never fight."

"Yeah, faggot to you. To me, he's a brutal bastard."

"Manny don't love you, Chica."

"He was pissed that you gave me a ride to bowling. Good thing he's not here today."

"He don't give a shit for Tito." He reached over and pulled Rachael closer. "He don't love you like I do."

Rachael put her hand onto Sanrio's crotch.

He smiled. "Chica, I want us together."

She snuggled closer. "Me too. I just worry about what Manny's gonna do—" She touched her bruised face without thinking.

"He ain't gonna do shit. Look what he did for Tito. Let him go to jail, *ayi yai yai*, he yelled. "If we were together, I could protect you both."

Rachael looked down at her hands and buffed the nails of one with the thumb of the other. Her eyebrows danced up and down several times. She was unsure.

~

The three falconers approached the pullout where they had parked their cars. Hayden and Grey dropped their packs by the Audi. Hayden unlocked the hatch and threw them in the back. Parker had opened the tailgate of his pickup and was taking his time getting the gyrfalcon into its cage. Grey and Hayden strolled a short distance.

The major had been thinking. "Carlysle? Why did y'all decide to gin up a program to save civilians?"

Hayden took a few moments to frame an answer. "NANCY is just the first step, major. Eventually, we want a system that will perform better, ethically, than human soldiers do in the battlefield."

"Whoa, you think the Army is ready for AWS?"

"The Army needs autonomous warfare systems," Hayden countered. "Look at the increasing tempo of warfare, the immense quantity of battlefield data, refinements in logic, and faster computer processing. It's inevitable: armies will deploy autonomous systems that can evaluate battlefield threats in realtime and respond with appropriate actions. Humans are no longer fast enough."

"Wait a second, Carlysle. The military has not said it's ethical to let a machine kill someone, has it?"

"The military already uses weapons systems that deploy lethal force autonomously, like the Navy's Phalanx system and its land-based counterpart, C-RAM. They are not considered unethical."

"But a live human deploys both of those systems," the major said.

"Yeah, but the machines decide what and when to shoot," Hayden replied. "If they inflict collateral damage, that's too bad. They have no way to avoid it. I think we can do better and that's what NANCY is about. War's become a political crime. Killing civilians is mass murder. I want to stop that."

"Indeed. That's why the Army is interested in your work, Carlysle."

"I designed NANCY to prevent the Army from taking innocent lives. She applies the highest possible standards of care to each mission and if she finds that probable civilian losses still outweigh the value of the target, she will abort the attack."

"Ah, the sanctity of human life, Carlysle. I agree, it is wrong to kill innocents, but in the mud and the smoke and the sand flies it's impossible to tell who's who."

"Major, NANCY can help the Army, but you must help us."

"Then tell me what you need because this zero tolerance thing is a pain in the pooper."

"NANCY assigns a potential risk to the human images she tracks. She adjusts that risk whenever she receives new information."

"That's why she staggers around like a blind horse in a pumpkin patch."

Hayden smiled. "Yes. She stumbles because we haven't given her enough information to decide where to go." He extended his left hand, palm up. "This is a group of civilians your soldiers encountered yesterday.. There were three possible outcomes"

Grey nodded. "Right. If they attacked, we were gonna retaliate. If they helped, we'd have welcomed them. But if they did nothing, that's when NANCY ought to have told us whether to hold our powder because we're hankering to shoot the wrong turkey."

Hayden stepped to the front of Parker's truck. "She can do that. NANCY keeps a record of each individual's actions in order to assign an immediate risk."

Grey walked with Hayden. "Then, what do you need from me?"

"NANCY decides whether to use lethal force according to military necessity," Hayden explained. "She must identify a legitimate combatant before she can tell you how to engage it in a way that avoids collateral damage. We need to know your willingness to let civilians die if NANCY misidentifies targets as combatants. In this case, a number between zero and one."

"Whoa. I can't do that, commit the Army to an absolute liability.
"

The two men contemplated each other.

"If I change the algorithms that protect civilians, your tactical commanders will have more flexibility. But I cannot assume that responsibility. You'd have to give me an official number."

Grey contemplated. "Carlysle, even if I could, that'd be a drastic change to the program by your strict ethics."

"Yes, it would."

"You beginning to see things through the fog of war?"

As Hayden considered the question, an image of Suzanne flashed through his mind. "Hard to say. I guess I'm a just little unsettled today."

"I hope your agitation doesn't hinder your ability to deliver NANCY to us on Friday."

Hayden doubted he would finish without the major's commitment, but said nothing.

Parker approached them. He had finished securing Merlin in his cage. "Gentlemen, I'm ready if you are." They both nodded to Parker and headed for the Audi.

～

After Hayden dropped the major at his car, he drove back to Los Alamos. No sooner was he on the road than Suzanne again haunted his thought. *How did she fall into the canyon? Tito? He hurt her. Was she trying to get away?* He felt anger swelling in his body and tried to calm himself. It was only when he drove past the lab he remembered again NANCY's looming deadline. He tried to concentrate on how to satisfy the Army and still maintain the moral integrity of his program. How to protect good people living in the umbras of ancient feuds? He hadn't found a solution by the time he pulled into the gas station and rolled to a stop at the pump island nearest the convenience store entrance. He stepped out, walked around to the pump, fed it his credit card, and inserted the fuel nozzle into the Audi's tank. With nothing to do but wait for the fill, he glanced around and noticed a familiar Chevy pickup parked on the far side of the gas station.

He remembered, *Christ, that was Manny's truck I almost hit.* He winced. *And I flipped him off.* A loud bang from the convenience store door broke his train of thought. He snapped his head toward the noise and saw Manny push through the door with one hand and drag Tito by the front of his shirt with the other.

Tito shouted at his father. "Let me go, asshole. I gotta class." The boy struggled but Manny spun him around and slammed him into a soda machine by the door.

"Whoa! What the fuck you think you're doing, boy."

"Leave me alone, asshole."

Hayden watched Manny cuff Tito's head and felt a tinge of satisfaction.

"Watch your mouth. I'm your father."

"You ain't shit."

Manny cuffed him again. "I said, watch your mouth."

"I'll watch what I want."

"What's up with you anyhow?"

Tito hissed at Manny. Even from fifteen feet away, Hayden heard the quiet menace in the boy's throat. "Suzanne, motherfucker. What do you think?"

Hayden felt the shock of Tito's words. He watched Manny release Tito's shirt and the boy dash immediately for the school. Manny stormed to the Chevy truck, got in, and tore out of the station.

Hayden replaced the fuel nozzle in the pump, walked around to the driver's door, and tried to force an image of Tito and his daughter from his thoughts.

~

Sanrio steered the monster truck around a steep uphill curve. His right foot was heavy on the gas and he was savoring the joy of pushing the suspension to its limit when suddenly Rachael startled him. "Watch out," she shouted. He had already glimpsed the cyclist standing on the shoulder of the highway. On second look, he saw the soiled racing gear and the crumpled bike beside him. He lifted his foot, the truck slowed, and Sanrio chuckled.

"Uh-oh, this hombre spilled. We're gonna give him a ride."

One side of Rachael's mouth curled in a sneer and she looked at the narrow space on seat between them. "Where are we supposed to put his weak Anglo ass? Can't even keep a bike on the road."

Sanrio glanced to the right with an easy smile and guided the truck to a stop just past the cyclist. "Cool it, Chica. The man needs help. He can ride in back."

The cyclist came alongside and peered through the glass of the passenger window with a relieved smile. Sanrio jerked his thumb to indicate he should ride in the truck bed.

~

Way-stations had occupied this turnout beside the highway for a very long time. The present incarnation, Grovenor's Stage Lines, had endured a century of rapacious owners. Its weathered structure retained a rugged charm despite periodic attempts to modernize it.

Hayden rolled the Audi past the wooden porch spanning the storefront and parked at the far end. As he entered the store, an unmuffled four-by-four rumbled into the parking lot outside. He peered between the hanging strands of chili *ristras* out the front windows and was mildly surprised to see Manny's wife, Rachael, slide out of the cab and storm over to the store. Each step of high heel boots stabbed the ground and sent shock waves oscillating through her full figure. She banged the screen and hurried to the register where Norma, her boss, waited with obvious irritation. Norma glanced at the watch on her large silver and turquoise bracelet. "Nice you could make it."

Rachael was in no mood for banter. She flashed a look of disgust and slipped the purse from her shoulder.

"Did you hear?" Norma crowed.

"What now?" Rachel braced for bad news.

"They're gonna widen the highway. I hope this place don't close."

Rachael flung her purse at a candy display. "That Sanrio don't know shit. Either that or he's fucking with me."

Norma backed away. "Jesus, Rachael. You two have a fight or something?"

Rachael glared at Norma then trudged over to the ruined display and disappeared from Hayden's line of sight when she bent down to collect the scattered sweets. Her voice floated up from beyond the canned soup.

"Yeah, and that Manny's getting wise, too. I don't know what I'll do if he finds out."

Moments later, Hayden left with a bag of charcoal under his right arm. The aluminum screen swung closed and the handle caught the bandage on his left hand with a solid yank. Hayden yelped, swung around and freed the bandage from the door.

He cradled his left arm and lowered himself into one of the wooden chairs on the porch. He unwound the gauze and looked at the red, throbbing line across his palm, held the hand in his lap and massaged around the swollen cut while memories of Suzanne ambushed his heart.

"Fucking Tito," he sighed.

With kneading, the pain in his hand diminished and Hayden rewound the bloody bandage. *How will I ever let this go?* he wondered. Hayden shook his head, picked up his charcoal, and walked to the Audi. The engine hummed to life and he shifted into gear. As the Audi turned onto the highway, he glimpsed the statue-like image of the forlorn cyclist, standing upright, shouldering his bent bike, waiting to be rescued.

~

Hayden parked in his driveway, opened the garage door for the far bay, dropped the charcoal by the wall and removed the tarp covering the ancient pickup. *Not cherry*, he thought. The original sea-green had worn away and exposed patches of rusted metal on the hood and fenders. The color of the doors reminded him of raw asparagus. He recalled how it swung around corners like a stage coach suspended on leather straps and stopped like a rocking-horse settling to rest. The antithesis of his tightly sprung Audi.

Hayden left the garage, pulled down the door, and checked the handle. He turned and saw Keith approaching from the street. He strode over to greet his son but he saw him stiffen as he neared. Keith tried to ignore him and headed to the porch. Hayden stopped him with his voice. "Hey, Keith. Did you hear? The sheriff let Tito walk."

"Yeah, I heard." He didn't seem surprised.

"That sit okay with you?"

"Yeah, I guess." He ascended the porch steps.

Hayden scoffed. At the sound, Keith turned and studied him. "Tito had nothing to do with Suzanne's accident, if that's what you're thinking."

"That's not what I heard."

"You heard wrong."

Hayden looked hard at Keith, who now loomed above him on the porch.

Keith stared back, unwavering. "If you heard anything different from what I just told you, it's wrong."

Hayden just smiled. Keith lowered his gaze, turned, and reached for the door handle.

Hayden knew the moment had passed. "All right. How are you doing otherwise?"

"Just keeping my focus, Dad. I got finals in a couple of weeks. Tomorrow I help Grandpa with the boat. Probably take us all day."

"What's the matter with the boat?"

Keith pulled open the door. "It came untied in that storm last Friday. The motor hit a rock. Cracked the transom. He wants to replace it." He stepped into the house.

"Good," Hayden said to his back. "Stay busy."

~

Hayden toasted two English muffins with green chilies and jack cheese, ate them, and then left home for his office at the lab. No one had restricted his security pass. He wondered how long that would last.

Sitting at his desk, with his feet up, gazing out the window, he chewed a pencil and thought about Friday's deadline. *Discrimination is the Army's problem. The major worries about distinguishing friend from foe when he cannot see the battlefield clearly. Human shortcomings limit his ability to discriminate. Therefore, he doesn't expect perfection. But NANCY can see from Space. Her abilities are beyond human. There is no need to reinterpret the criterion, loosen the distinction between combatants and non-combatants, but it's what he wants me to do.*

Hayden wondered whether his judgment was growing cloudy. *Jesus, talk about the fog of war.* Yet, the more he thought over the puzzle the more obscure the answers seemed, the more confused he became, and the more concerned he was with finding a solution. *I've only got two more days.*

His attention shifted absently to the metal box, the *objet d'art*, he had completed in his garage. It stood prominently on his desk. No one could miss it. He was about to pick up the threads of his problem when his office door opened and Holly, his young assistant, entered with a stack of papers in her arms.

"Mr. Davis sent these over for your review," she set the papers in the desk and admired the shiny metal box. "Oh, that's your new lunch box."

Hayden eyed the pile of work. "Yes it is. Like it?"

Holly regarded the object as if it was an item on sale. "Well, it certainly is well made." She offered a neutral smile.

Hayden wasn't offended. "I wanted something different."

She stood and waited.

"Holly?" Hayden read her thoughts.

"Well," she paused and glanced down at the floor. "I was talking with Maryanne over at county. She said that Manny's boy, Tito, got in trouble last summer for beating up a girl in Jémez Springs." She raised her eyes. "I don't...well...I thought you'd want to know."

Hayden felt a rush of adrenaline. His face turned white. He stammered. "Thanks, Holly. I didn't know." He tried to show appreciation by smiling but it came out as a grimace. He indicated with a wave that they she could leave.

Her relief was palpable. "You're welcome."

Hayden watched her close the office door. He stared after her for a long while, motionless, his eyes dark and unfocused as he pictured Suzanne running through sagebrush away from her aggressor. He saw the look of fear on her face.

~

Later that afternoon, after he had arrived home, Hayden went to his small office and spent nearly an hour reviewing the materials Parker had sent, but made little progress. The pressure of Friday's deadline had knotted the muscles in his neck and shoulders and given him a headache. No wonder he couldn't concentrate. He longed for Suzanne. Finally, he stood and walked to his daughter's room and sat on the bed, hoping he would feel something of her, but the void inside him remained empty, without connection. She wasn't. He took her diary from the bedside table and began flipping pages, marveled at the skill of her drawing. Her writing seemed real and unreal at the same time: her words but none he'd ever heard spoken.

He was looking at me again. I wasn't even doing anything. Talking to Marsha about going out with Patrick on Saturday. Patrick's dad lets him use the car. She wants it so bad.

Hayden turned the page. On the left-hand side he saw a skillful rendering of a boy slouching in a chair, leaning back on two legs with his foot against a library table. On the right, a few lines of text.

Too full of himself. Marsha says I'll never get him. She doesn't know I've got a secret.

Hayden wondered briefly about the secret then flipped the page. The left-hand side showed a boy, full face, instantly recognizable as Tito. On the right, one word in elaborate script "Gorgeous."

Hayden's bandaged hand pressed the open book in his lap. The fingers of his right hand caressed the lettering.

His eyes filled with tears. He moved the book so he wouldn't stain it. He scrunched his face and fought the familiar but out-of-place words that leaped to his mind, NANCY's engagement criteria: "Using lethal force requires upholding all forbidden constraints and having at least one obligation to act." Suddenly, he wondered. *How is this different?*

Hayden sat in her room most of the afternoon trying to sort through his confusion. In the evening, Lucy called him to dinner. When they had finished, he cleared the dinner dishes from the table. She rinsed and filled the dish washer.

"I know this is last minute," he said. "But I can't go to dinner at your brother's on Thursday"

"So Keith and I will have to stand in for you?"

"I've got too much to do."

"Well, I just thought—'

He interrupted, "I know you were counting on me and I'm sorry but I've got a deadline on Friday."

I just hope you'll be able to clear your mind, Hayden." Her concern sounded genuine but before he could respond, the jarring buzz of his mobile interrupted them. He put down the dishes and answered. "Carlysle," he said.

He heard Parker's voice. "Good evening, Hayden. I called because I had an inspiration."

"Sounds dangerous."

"It is. You know we have access to the Army's satellite imagery. I'll bet you could ask Major Grey to let you examine the records for Burnt Mesa. Who knows? You might see something."

"Will he let me?"

"Aren't you two friends?"

"Very good, Parker. I'll call him."

"How you coming along for Friday?"

"I'll make it," Hayden returned the mobile to his pocket. Lucy stopped rinsing and looked at him. "What's he want now?"

The question surprised him."Huh? Oh, just reminded me of Friday's deadline."

"I thought the lab put you on ice until they reviewed the accident."

"They did. But the Army doesn't stop and I can't either"

~

Major Grey agreed to meet at the Uplink Center. When Hayden strode into the darkened room, he was surprised to see it fully occupied at the late hour. He supposed that someone had to keep tabs on the moving images piped in from around the world.

He found the major working a keyboard before a big screen monitor. He took a chair beside him and watched images fast-forward across the screen. He saw numerals rolling over like a speedometer, saw it was the date, and recognized the search area. He guided Grey.

"Yeah, yeah. No. Back one day. Good. That's it."

Grey hit a key and the blur stopped. The monitor showed a composite-infrared image of Northern New Mexico. Grey's finger pointed to a spot on the screen. "Here's where we are." He made some adjustments on the keyboard and the image zoomed progressively larger, showing terrain, then highways. Grey repositioned the image and pointed with his finger. "This is Los Alamos. This is Bandelier. Where exactly are we going?"

Hayden touched the screen with his forefinger. "There. That's Burnt Mesa."

Grey again repositioned the view and zoomed in until they saw rocks and sagebrush. "What time, Carlysle?"

"About 8:45, as I recall."

The major entered the time on the keyboard and the image blurred while the computer searched. When the picture stabilized, the men saw two human figures: one still, a second moving in circles.

"Son of a bitch!" Hayden's surprise carried across the quiet room. No one reacted.

Onscreen, the still figure moved to edge of the precipice and stopped. Minutes later the circling figure joined it. At the same time, a ring of distortion, slightly smaller than the human figures, appeared on the screen by the cliff a short distance away. Like a turbulent cloud it traveled toward the human figures blurring the sharp details in the underlying image as it passed over them. The movement caught Grey's attention.

"Will you look at that," Grey said, genuinely amazed. "What the hell is that?"

Hayden looked at Grey. "Damned if I know."

They watched the blur move toward the human forms and, when it joined them, all three merged, like puddles of spilled liquid, into a single ghostly image.

The distortion churned slowly for several moments before it resolved into a lone human figure that walked away from the cliff, leaving no sign of the other.

The two men sat motionless, eyes fixed on the monitor, stunned. After several moments, the major asked, "What just happened?"

Hayden swiveled his chair around to face at him. "I can't explain."

"That blur?" Grey's pitch rose.

"No idea," Hayden replied.

Grey stared into the monitor. "You ever heard the expression, I feel like I been ate by a wolf and shit over a cliff?"

Hayden's mind was straining to interpret the images he'd just seen.

Still looking at the monitor, Grey said,, "This is a multispectral view in the visible and near-infrared band and we've got very high rate image telemetry." He concentrated. "What do they call it when certain energy beams interact to create a frequency shift in the signal?"

"The Wolf Effect," Hayden looked at the screen. "After the physicist who discovered it"

"Could that be what we saw?"

Hayden shook his head. "I don't know. But I do know that I saw two people at the start and only one walked away."

The major turned to Hayden. "You think the one walked away was that boy?"

"That son of a bitch." Hayden cut him off in a burst of self-righteous feeling.

~

Hayden stormed into the kitchen and found Lucy waiting. She must have sensed his fervor because she stepped right into his path. He stopped, hoping to avoid conversation and should have known better.

"I'm worried about you." She tried to find his eyes.

He looked past her, over her head. "I'm all right."

"You can't hide from me."

"I'm okay, really."

She came closer, reached up, and took his head in both hands and pulled it down to face hers.

"Hayden, I know you. You become obsessed."

When he tried to pull away, she restrained him. "Don't lose control of yourself"

Hayden gave a small shake of his head.

"Even Keith thinks you're focused too much on Tito." She lowered her head to see up into his downcast eyes. He shook his head again. She tightened her grip and rocked his head with concerned affection. "Please. I see shadowy impulses in those eyes."

Hayden composed a friendly face. "My dear doctor of philosophy. I know what I'm doing."

"Hayden," she said. "You design machines that have no emotion clouding their judgment when they distinguish soldiers from innocents. But you are a man. You do have emotions."

"I am," he acknowledged.

"I worry that your emotions will overpower you reason."

"They won't," he said, turning away and she let go.

～

Hayden lay awake. Lucy breathed soundly beside him while his mind raced in circles, chasing down Tito. In the dark, his tortured soul ignited a steady panorama of depraved spectacles and staged them in the theater of his imagination. He tasted acid in the back of his throat every time he imagined the boy with his daughter on the edge of the mesa.

From time to time, Lucy's words forced NANCY's programming into his thoughts: "Lethal force...uphold all forbidden constraints...have at least one obligation to act."

So, what is forbidden?

Tito was an aggressor, now properly identified.

Where is the obligation to act?

"An eye for an eye." It's as old as history.

Do I have legitimate authority?

He took the life of an innocent. My innocent. My family. What more authority do I need?

Have I taken all feasible precautions to minimize the loss of human life?

Bullshit, Hayden. You heard him in the jail; he hurt her. He beat up a girl in Jémez Springs. You saw him with Suzanne on the mesa and watched her disappear from the edge.

Well, at least I could talk to him.

For Christ's sake, get on with it.

Wednesday

~

Hayden sat behind the wheel of the old green pickup and drove away from the afternoon sun at a lazy thirty miles per hour, unaware of the engine's smooth purr or the suspension's gentle sway.

He was dazed from the lack of sleep and couldn't say why he was driving or what he intended. He knew only that sometime during the long night he'd decided he must talk with Tito. He guessed that the boy would take the old road home after school. The traffic was slower and less frequent but more likely to give him a ride than the fast moving cars on the highway. When he saw Tito walking on the shoulder ahead with his thumb out, Hayden felt his stomach roil. He shifted in his seat, looked behind him. No other vehicles on the road.

He slowed the truck and glided to a stop beside Tito. The boy turned, looked in the open passenger window and recognized Hayden. His face clouded with suspicion for an instant before the oddball truck provoked a curious smile. "Mr. Carlysle! Where'd you get this old beater?"

"Someone in the family," Hayden said.

Tito laughed and reached for the door handle. "Must've been someone old. You sure we'll get there?"

"No problem," Hayden said.

Tito pulled open the door and climbed into the cab. Hayden watched him over the angular metal lunchbox resting on the seat between them. The boy swiveled in the seat, grabbed the door handle and pulled it closed. He sat back and smiled.

"How old is this thing, anyway?"

Hayden shrugged.

Tito noticed the sculpture on the seat between them, pointed with his thumb. "What's that?"

"My lunchbox," he replied.

"Nice. Looks like a relic from Worlds of Warcraft."

"I wanted something different."

"Cool." He paused and looked at Hayden. "Where's Keith today?"

"He's home."

"He okay?"

Hayden rocked his head from side to side, pushed the floor shift into first, and let out the clutch. The truck moved forward and Hayden decided to come right to the point. But before he could speak, Tito turned to him.

"Mr. Carlysle, I'm sorry about Suzanne. I know how much she —"

Hayden released the gear lever and knifed his right hand up in the air between them, cut him off with a sharp, "I know." The abruptness startled the boy.

After a long silence, Tito said. "I really liked her. She was so beautiful."

Hayden seethed inside but kept his eyes on the road. He tried again to ask Tito about Suzanne, but again the boy spoke first.

"I saw her and Keith all the time in Bandelier."

Hayden was fuming at the second interruption and barely heard what Tito said. "I didn't know that."

Tito looked at him with a troubled expression. "Yeah, last time was on Burnt Mesa." He looked away, almost in tears. "Makes me sad to think of her."

Hayden felt the lie, felt himself grow cold. A tiny fiber snapped deep inside and he stepped instantly, cleanly, through a threshold he never knew existed. He steered onto the shoulder and slowed the truck to a stop.

Tito was suddenly alert. "Why are we stopping?"

Hayden choked on the words. "Something I want to show you." He saw the nervous look, the questioning in the boy's eyes. His own body moved as if it belonged to someone else. He lifted the lunchbox by the handle with his right hand and drew it back across his chest. He kept his body and mind relaxed and neutral, gave away nothing.

Suddenly, blindly, Hayden let his body snap. His right arm lashed around in an arc and slammed the metal box into Tito's face.

Hayden felt blood splatter into his eyes, saw Tito's hands fly to his head, heard a scream. It supercharged him. He landed another vicious swing. Saw the angular weapon lacerate the little fucker's head. Knock him back into the seat.

Another swing with all his might. It made him feel giddy. Again. Euphoric. And again. And again. And again. Tito's body bounced with each blow until finally it fell limp and still. Hayden dropped the box, shook his head and filled the air with a savage yell of triumph and rage. Emotion contorted his face. Spittle streaked the windshield.

Slowly, the gasping receded and the luster drained from his eyes. The wolfish grin slackened to a frown. He looked over at the body. Nausea filled his stomach. As if he had just realized where he was, he glanced out the rear window, then through the windshield. No one in sight. Still, he felt a sudden urgency. Anxiety smothered his judgment. His reason unraveled like a cut hawser.

Hayden reached over the bloody corpse and pushed open the passenger door. He leaned back, placed his right foot against the body and shoved.

A broken Tito crumpled onto the dusty shoulder. One hand struck the ground, fell open, and a wolf fetish dropped out. It rolled and bounced into a sagebrush.

Hayden pulled the door closed, revved the engine, and lurched from the shoulder, spraying pebbles over the dusty, bloody dirt.

～

The ancient pickup steered itself into a parking space by the entry to the sheriff's office. It stopped. The engine turned off. Hayden let his hands fall to his lap, looked around him at the blood splattered on the windows, the headliner, the seat, his clothes, and his hands; he looked in the mirror, on his face.

He listened to a voice in his head tell him to get out of the truck, go inside, and tell Tom what he'd just done. His left hand reached for the door handle, found the cold chrome, and stopped. It floated back to the steering wheel. The voice said, *Tom, I can't believe what I just did. I lost control and avenged my daughter.* His hand reached once more for the handle but stopped again. He shook his head. The voice said, *Wait. He deserved it.*

His right hand reached down and turned the ignition key, his left pressed the starter button.

~

Hayden drove the truck east, across the Rio Grande, turned south onto Shumaa Road, and continued over Pueblo Lands until he found an isolated arroyo. He parked in a stand of cottonwoods where he doubted anyone would ever see the truck. Anxiety had abandoned him during the drive, remorse quickly filled the vacancy and he rolled the past hour's events over in his mind. *How did that happen? You were going to talk to him. Something inside me snapped. Right, and you really cleared up the case for security, too. They'll surely let you finish NANCY now. Well, screw them if they don't. Without emotion, there's no justice. It's in our blood. The history of human conflict.*

Hayden reached behind the seat for some rags and a bottle of solvent but stopped on seeing the blood spattered interior. Fear percolated in his chest and he thought of Lucy. *Oh my god. What will happen when she finds out?* He didn't move for several moments. He had no answer. He retrieved the cleaning supplies, thought, *Well, shit. What's done is done.* He began removing the red stains from the interior. Two hours later he buried his bloodied garments, cleaned himself and dressed in old clothes he kept in the trunk. As he began the long trudge to the highway, he thought, *Some part of you must have known. You drove the pickup today not the Audi.*

~

Tom Winston had seen death. He'd seen brutality. Tito's head almost made him lose his *rellenos.* He'd have given ten dollars for a beer and looked at his colleagues to see if one might be forthcoming, but neither Deputy Rodriguez nor the four other officers hovering around Tito's body showed the slightest concern. The coroner, squatting beside the corpse, couldn't be expected to feel anything either nor add any illuminating facts beyond the obvious as it turned out.

"Multiple blows to the head. To the face. Very straightforward. Very violent."

"Still warm," Winston added.

"Less than two hours, I'd say."

"Okay. We got the photos. He's yours," Winston said.

The coroner looked behind him to his assistant resting his butt on the flat bed of the hearse. It must have been a signal between them because the assistant immediately pulled the stretcher from the back, laid a body bag on top, and wheeled it toward his boss.

Tom didn't feel right. It wasn't his stomach, it was something else. Something he didn't understand about this crime. "Look around, boys. See if there's anything we missed."

Four officers fanned out to search the area again. Tom grabbed Deputy Rodriguez by the shirt sleeve before he could join in the search. "Rusty, walk with me."

The deputy shrugged and changed direction.

"So? Whaddya think?" The sheriff pressed on.

"Next of kin always tops the list. Right, chief?"

The coroner and his assistant moved the two policemen aside so they could collect the corpse and load it into their vehicle. The sheriff and his deputy strolled along the shoulder.

"Yeeaah, I'm not sure," Winston said.

"Why not?"

"The kid wasn't getting on with his old man. Teenage rebellion. But I know his wife loved him."

"Carlysle?"

Winston turned to Rusty. "On account of the kid being involved with his daughter? Thought he had something to do with her death?"

Rusty nodded.

"He's more brainiac than maniac."

"I saw him with the daughter after she fell," Rusty said. "Guy was devastated."

Winston considered it. "Yup. We'll check him out."

"An act of random violence?" the deputy offered.

Winston suppressed a smile. "Remind me again, when is it you plan on taking the detective's exam?"

~

Manny slouched with his back against the split-rail fence that ran in front of his house and watched the sheriff's car pull away to his right. He sagged helplessly into a squat beside the road, put his elbows on his knees, and dropped his head into his hands. His body shook with every sob.

The sobs became moans. The moans turned into wails. Manny struggled to his feet, walked around the end of the fence into his yard and tromped in circles, hands alternately on his head or waving in the air, fists clenching and unclenching. The wails merged into a continuous cry of pain.

From the adjoining yard, his cousin Xavier heard the racket and thrust his head over the cedar hedge between them.

Xavier asked in Spanish, "Cousin, what happened? Did your wife come home early?"

Manny either didn't hear or chose to ignore the jibe because he continued circling and wailing.

"C'mon bro. What's wrong?" Xavier asked, more sympathetic this time. Manny still didn't respond. Xavier came around the hedge into Manny's yard, caught up with him and shouted in his face. "Manny! What the fuck is the matter?"

Manny looked at Xavier as if seeing him for the first time. He stumbled to him, threw his arms over his cousin's shoulders, and went slack. Xavier was caught off guard but got Manny's weight under control and stood stiff and expressionless.

"Tito, Man." Manny's Spanish came out between sobs. "Tito. He's dead."

Xavier blinked like he didn't hear right.

"Somebody bashed his head," Manny wailed.

Xavier understood, his eyes moistened, he embraced his cousin and began to moan with him. "Oh, my God." Soon he released Manny, who let Xavier guide him around the hedge toward his home. He called ahead to his wife. "Julieta! Julieta, come quick."

Julieta came running out the front door, wiping her hands on her apron. She stopped when she saw Xavier leading Manny by the arm toward their house. Xavier commanded her, "Tito's been killed. Call everyone. Tell them to come."

Julieta's face fell. She turned pale. A second later, she nodded and ran back into the house. Xavier kept Manny moving slowly, painfully toward his front door.

Inside their home, Julieta erected a line of card tables and chairs from the kitchen into the living room. Within minutes, relatives had arrived and covered the tables with their stock of leftovers: *rellenos*, *tamales*, chili, tortilla pie, *pasole, carne asada*, salsa, corn, roast pork, venison, cakes, fruit, and eggs. More than a dozen people now commiserated with Manny. Sitting, standing, eating, drinking. Manny drank a beer, not his first. His brown face was red and streaked, his eyes swollen and moist. He soaked up the attention, acted gracious, but inside it mattered not. Grief crushed his heart in its bulldog jaws.

Uncle Diego sat on one side, Aunt Isabella on the other, and they drank with him, ribbed him, and tried to distract him from the pain.

"Remember that time on the Pecos?" Diego recalled. Other relatives gathered around Manny, encouraged him, touched him, and talked gently in his ear.

Isabella took up the story. "You kept yelling for Tito."

Manny struggled with a bleak smile.

"You dropped your pole and jumped in after it," Diego laughed. Everyone laughed.

"You were gonna drown," Isabella laid a warm hand on Manny's shoulder. More laughter. Manny showed them his red bleary eyes.

"We had to chase you half a mile before we fished you out," Diego joked. "You were the biggest thing anybody caught all day."

Of course, it wasn't working. Manny put his hands on the table, stood, and bawled. "I can't keep thinking about him." He stumbled over the chair and staggered out the kitchen door in a daze. They understood and watched him go.

Outside, Manny weaved a crooked path through Xavier's yard into his own. He stumbled to his truck, opened the door, removed his keys, and crawled into the driver's seat. He fumbled the key into the ignition and started the engine, but before he could put the truck in gear, his head lolled backwards onto the headrest. His eyes stared up at the headliner briefly and then closed.

Memories played in his head like a dream. In it, he sat in the parked truck behind the wheel. One arm rested along the top of the seat back. He felt hot and sweaty, *la verga* throbbed painfully in his crotch. He looked next to him at Suzanne in the passenger seat, wearing a short skirt and halter. Her eyes alternated between assertive and fearful.

"Why are we stopped?" she demanded.

He turned his body towards her hoping she'd react to his burning lust. "I just want to look at you."

Her laugh sounded weak. "You see me every Sunday in church."

"Today, you are more beautiful than I have ever seen you, Suzanne."

"Is that why you gave me a ride?"

He slid closer. Desire seethed from his pores. "I was hoping we could become better friends."

He caught her nauseated look. "Oh like what, hookup or something?"

He reached his left hand, cradled her right breast.

"Mr. Montoya! What are you doing?" She moved her hand to push his away.

His right arm pulled her closer.

"Mr. Montoya! Stop! Are you crazy? I do not want this."

His left hand tore away her halter.

"Stop. You're hurting me." She tried to push away. He felt her anger and panic, her fists on his head and shoulders, but he couldn't take his eyes off her naked, trembling breasts. "Stop it!" she screamed. "Damn you! I said, Stop! Nooo!"

~

Manny could not remember driving to the Blue Lantern Tavern or sitting at the bar or anything besides the awful sadness. He slumped, on a stool by himself, before a row of empty shot glasses and a stack of bills on the dark wooden bar.

The bartender, Rollo, stood in front of him with a bottle of tequila and two shot glasses. He placed the glasses on the bar, poured the drinks, and pulled a bill from the pile. In the distance, Manny heard the front door open but didn't look up. He didn't see Jose, Rachael's girlfriend, come in the door and take the empty stool beside him. She removed her jacket, swung around to face him and displayed her abundant décolletage. He was still hovering over his drinks and missed the show but her voice penetrated the haze. "Hi Manny. You all alone? C'mon and buy me a drink."

It wasn't time to wake from the dull stupor. He didn't even look at her. "Not if you're gonna sit and peck at me like a sour hen."

"Manny!" She sounded hurt. "Gimme a break. I sat here to be nice. Have a little fun, you know?"

Anything to shut her up. He signaled the bartender who raised his eyebrows in question. He pointed to Jose.

"Thank you!" she said. "That's more like it."

Rollo glanced at Jose for her order. She pointed at Manny's shot glasses and nodded. The bartender stepped away to get the tequila bottle. Before he could return with a glass and pour, Jose helped herself to Manny's second full glass. Manny gave Rollo a whaddya-gonna-do expression. The bartender poured another shot and placed it in the line of Manny's glasses.

Jose leaned close and Manny felt her soft chest press against his arm. "So, Rachael's not here. We can get into trouble tonight."

He couldn't imagine it. "Rachael's still at work. Afraid I'm not going to be much fun tonight."

"What's the matter, hon. Still blue about that Carlysle girl?"

He straightened, shook his head in disbelief. "Jose, you are a piece of work."

She reached over and took the shot Rollo had poured for Manny, drew it to her lips, and gave him a big smile. "I know. Men love it."

He swiveled the stool and trained his red face directly at hers. "You didn't hear about Tito?"

She had the glass poised at her mouth. "What about him?" She sipped.

"Sheriff found his body this afternoon. Somebody bashed his head."

Jose's eyes widened. Her mouth opened mid-sip. Tequila poured down the front of her blouse, between her ample breasts. Manny turned to Rollo idling nearby and made a pouring motion with his hand. The bartender brought a bottle, poured another for Jose, and two for Manny.

Manny returned to the slump, head bowed over the glasses, eyes glazed. "I've done bad things, Jose. Things I'm ashamed of. Hurt some really good people."

Jose grabbed a bar napkin and concentrated on cleaning her blouse. "Tito! My God, Manny. I had no idea."

"God is punishing me," he almost sobbed.

She was busy scrubbing the soaked fabric. "Manny, I'm so sorry for you."

"Tito...dead...it's my payback."

He turned and saw she was still pushing her chest around with a napkin. Without taking her eyes from her stained blouse, she said, "I heard strange things about Tito. You don't think his dying had anything to do with the Carlysle girl, do you?"

Manny sat up like he'd received a shot of caffeine. "Now there's a question. I been wondering myself. I need an answer." He stood, swayed and staggered for the door.

Jose put the frayed napkin on the bar, watched Manny leave, and turned to Rollo. "Ain't this just fucking great!"

Rollo smiled, grabbed the tequila bottle, and ambled over to her. She watched him pour another shot then leaned forward to pick up the glass. He watched the dark line between her breasts widen to a tawny valley as gravity pulled them apart.

~

Hayden arrived home well past the dinner hour. Lucy cooked a sparse meal, which they ate at the kitchen table. He avoided her eyes.

"Keith is making the awakening ceremony," she said with pride.

Hayden didn't conceal his skepticism."What will that do?"

His tone irked her. "You used to have faith in my family's traditions, Hayden. You know, thousands of years in passing along the lessons of life."

Hayden placed his fork beside his plate. He looked down at the unfinished meal and felt trapped. How would he ever get NANCY finished in time? How would he deal with his family? He could justify revenge to himself. But he knew Lucy could never accept murder. He could risk telling her and lose the rest of his family or say nothing and cause an insurmountable barrier to grow between them like a cancer. He hated both alternatives, but there was no going back. He had to choose. "Listen, the thing with Tito?" he began, "We need to talk about it—"

The doorbell interrupted him. Lucy closed her eyes, frustrated, and let her hands fall to the table.

"I'll get it," Hayden said and pushed back his chair.

Opening the front door, Hayden was surprised and puzzled to see Manny, bleary eyed and swaying precariously on the stoop. "Manny?"

He received an unfocused stare and an pathetic attempt to control slurring speech. "Hayden, I'm not bothering you?"

"It's okay, Manny," he said, uncertain. "What's up?"

"Can we talk?"

Hayden stepped past Manny onto the porch and looked around the yard. He saw nothing extraordinary. He faced Manny. "Sure," he said, putting one hand on his shoulder and holding the door open for him.

Manny stumbled into the room, turned to Hayden and blurted, "You heard about Tito?"

Hayden tried to look neutral. "Yes, I did. I'm sorry."

The hurt in Manny's eyes was painful to see. "Both our kids, man. Friends. Just days apart."

Hayden managed to appear sympathetic. He gestured for them to sit. Manny didn't acknowledge, but moved closer to Hayden and smothered him in a reek of tequila.

"I figured we could talk."

"Sure." He hid his revulsion. "Go ahead, Manny."

Again the slur, "Lemme ask you something. You think there's a connection?"

Hayden opened his mouth but shut it again when he saw Lucy enter from the kitchen. She walked up to Manny and took his arm in both hands.

"Manny, that was you at the door." She saw his distress. "Are you all right?"

For a moment, her touch tamed his rage. "Yeah...it's just...Tito."

"I know. I'm so sorry."

Manny backed away and the menace returned, "S'ugly, s'what it is."

She folded her arms. "What did Tom say?"

"Nothing."

She looked at Hayden. "Just like with Suzanne."

Manny stumbled and began to pace a circle around the room. Hayden saw the drunken anger rise with each wobbly step, knew just how he felt.

"I'm fucking insane, Hayden."

"I know."

"It's getting to me."

"Yeah, you just want to kill someone." Hayden's own anger rushed to his face. The words made Manny turn and glare at him but he continued to walk.

"I'm this far," Manny held up his right hand and fumbled with the thumb and forefinger until they were half an inch apart. "From taking some motherfucker to pieces."

Hayden knew of Manny's reputation for violence, yet he stood passive and watched him come around the living room toward him. Manny stopped in front of Hayden and leaned nose to nose. "You didn't hurt Tito. Did you?"

Hayden remained calm, unsurprised and unafraid. But not Lucy. The insinuation appalled her. "Manny!"

"No," Hayden said quickly when he saw her react.

Manny continued to glare at him. "Work today?"

Lucy stepped next to them and looked at Hayden.

"Yes," Hayden said. "On my computer. All afternoon."

Manny took a half step back. His face was flushed. He looked at a spot on the wall over Hayden's shoulder.

"Awe, man. The two of them. It's just too much coincidence."

Hayden wanted to ease him down. "Manny—"

Manny thundered a solid left hook into Hayden's ribcage. He almost fell to the carpet. The pain in his side made him want to vomit, he couldn't breathe. He doubled over and tried to inhale.

Lucy went rigid. "Manny! What are you doing?" she screamed. Might as well have been in the next house. He didn't hear her.

Hayden tilted his head up and saw Manny crouching before him, his face twisted and his fists clenched. "Coincidence. You know what I mean, Hayden?"

He felt another explosion of pain as Manny again drove a left fist into his ribs, "Don't you?"

Hayden stumbled, gulped like a fish, couldn't take a breath.

Lucy grabbed Manny's arm. "Manny! Stop! We're heartbroken over Tito."

He turned his drunkard's vacant grin in her direction. After a long moment his eyes focused and he recognized her. "Lucy, Lucy. I'm...I'm sorry. I gotta go."

She stepped back to let him pass. He staggered to the front door.

Hayden had his lungs working, but couldn't stand. He cautiously turned his head and saw Manny lean on the door jam and look back at him. "Swear to God, Hayden."

He coughed. "I swear." And was relieved to see Manny disappear out the front door.

~

Sanrio descended the concrete steps from the street into Rosie's all-night diner. He entered and saw a bored teenage waitress behind the fountain and her only customer, Rachael, sitting in one of the red vinyl booths. Her right hand was on the Juke box, flipping the metal tabs to turn pages of the music library. He approached and she gave him an empty glance. As he slid into the seat across from her, she asked, "Hear about Tito?"

"Yeah, they found his body on the highway by the old fab building."

Her demeanor was cloudy, dismayed, not perky like he was used to. "You don't know how many times I told that boy not to hitchhike."

"I'm sorry for him."

She bit her fist. "He was my only son. My beautiful boy."

"Are you okay?"

"I'm fucked."

He smiled. "We can fix that."

The waitress arrived and stood beside the table.

"Coffee for me," Sanrio said.

Rachael smiled. "Just a refill." She waited for the server to leave. "I don't know what Manny's doing."

"What do you mean?"

"I mean he's crazy. Can't think straight. He's no good to anyone."

Sanrio thought for a moment. "Ah, Chica. What does this mean for us?"

She wasn't in a mood to speculate. "Machuque, I don't know. Why you ask me all these questions?"

He reached across the table with his right hand. "Look. He didn't protect that boy, did he?"

"No."

He took her forearm. "He's not helping you?"

"Sure as shit."

"Gotta head full of grief?"

"Yeah."

"Maybe his mind is somewhere else?"

"Yeah."

"He doesn't see what's happening around him?"

"Yeah?"

His hand shook her forearm for emphasis. "Chica, now is the time."

Rachael sighed. She closed her eyes and dropped her chin to her chest.

The waitress brought a cup and a pot of coffee. They watched her in silence pour coffee and leave.

Rachael regarded him from across the table. "What are you thinking of?"

"What do you think I'm thinking of?"

He watched tears well in her eyes. She asked him again, "What are you thinking?"

Women! he thought to himself. *Always crying. Always playing innocent.* "Don't be a dumb shit. You know what I'm thinking. Are you ready, is all."

Her lips moved but words didn't come. He barely heard her second try. "Yeah. I guess."

"Good." He sat back with both hands on the table. "Now listen, Chica. Who would want to hurt your boy?"

She no longer fought the tears. "I don't know."

"Didn't the sheriff say Tito had something to do with that girl dying at Bandelier?"

"That's what Manny said."

He found her eyes with his own and said in a low voice, "Maybe it was her father killed Tito."

She looked at him with surprise. "What? Like revenge?"

"Yeah!"

"No. You think so?"

How could she not see? It was blindingly obvious. "Not what I think. What the law thinks. If they believe Manny is looking to avenge Tito by killing the scientist and Manny gets shot, who are they gonna blame?"

She was like a child. "Who?"

He didn't believe it. "The scientist, Chica! The scientist."

"Machuque, my head hurts."

He took a sip of his coffee and tried to relax."Okay. Okay. Chica. I got it all worked out. Just take it easy."

Rachael scanned anxiously around the diner. He thought she looked fearful.

Thursday

~

Keith waited in the living room for Somoma. The stone fireplace had not yet burned off the morning chill so he toasted his backside in the radiant heat, studied a large abstract painting that dominated the opposite wall. The room's other walls were whitewashed adobe while the ceiling and the floor were dark polished wood. Apart from the painting, the only color came from a bright woven rug that seemed to float on the gleaming floor.

Keith felt Somoma next to him, saw that he carried two steaming cups. "Shaman, what is this painting?"

Somoma regarded the painting. "An artist in Taos painted that. He was a white man. He gave it to my uncle many years ago. Uncle threw it in the dump. I saved it because I thought it would help me see the wolf in my dreams."

"Does it?"

Somoma shook his head. "It was painted by a white man. He never saw a wolf."

Keith studied the painting again. "It's hard for me to see anything."

"Yes, but it is good for dreaming." Somoma handed him one of the cups and gestured to the woven rug. "Sit. Drink this. We will begin."

Keith stepped onto the rug and lowered himself into a cross-legged position. Somoma did the same. Together, they faced the painting and sipped their tea.

"I will go with you," said the Shaman. "You will not see me. Do not look for me. I cannot help you. It is your dream."

This information did not add to Keith's confidence. He was already anxious with the anticipation of a challenging adventure. He looked at Somoma. The Shaman raised his cup as a sign to drink.

When they had finished their tea, Somoma reached into his pocket and removed a handful of finely ground blue powder and threw it over Keith. The youth smiled at Somoma and then they stared into the artwork together.

"Shaman, I wish to say something."

Somoma grunted to indicate he was listening.

"Suzanne and I had a friend. Some people thought he killed her. He was murdered."

"Mm." Somoma stared into the painting. "Perhaps you will find the answer when you dream."

Keith returned his attention to the painting. He felt his chest grow warm. The white room grew dark. The shiny floor disappeared. Deep in the painting, pigments unwound, strands of color spiraled to the surface, drifting like smoke into the room. Bright hues enveloped him in fanciful fingers of joy and drew him into their bosom. He fell, adrift, tumbling among crazy, intimate shapes.

The dream felt real, as if he was watching the sunrise over Frijoles Canyon. Dawn's brilliance flooded the high desert with throbbing orange, overwhelming the saturated greens and blues.

Yet, it can't be real. He knew wolves didn't live nearby, but he was watching a huge grey lope along the edge of the canyon. It halted, alert, and glared at two squirrels by a Ponderosa pine.

It moved and the squirrels fled. The wolf resumed its gait along the cliff, searched the sagebrush and then stopped and cocked its ears. Keith watched it slink toward the brink with its head low. Without warning, it lunged at a human figure leaning away, over the cliff. It didn't land on the shape but merged with it as if they were two columns of smoke.

Suddenly, Keith was inside that swirling image. Suzanne was there too. He looked down into her tearstained face. They hung in midair over the chasm for several moments and then fell, staring silently into each other's eyes. The world spun, the river below revolved like a lost compass needle. Keith felt nauseous, tried to cry out to Suzanne but couldn't catch his breath. They were about to smash onto the rocks when the fall suddenly stopped. Disoriented by the abrupt stillness, he waited until his brain refocused and then found himself sitting cross legged on a dirt floor in the center of a low round chamber. His eyes burned. The air was hot, tinged with the smell of wood smoke. The only sound was an occasional crackle from the fire by his side. He rubbed his eyes and tried to see. When his sight could finally penetrate the smoke he encountered one ferocious countenance after another glaring down at him from atop the squat logs buried on end around the perimeter. His mind told him they were Indians in ceremonial dress, colored paints, feathers, skins, beads, jewelry, their heads encased in grotesque masks, abstractions of their animal spirits: Badger, Bear, Cougar, Coyote, Eagle, Hawk, Snake, Squirrel, Wolf. All different. All terrifying.

Yet their voices materialized inside his head in the unambiguous language of his ancestors, Keres. Unspoken words drew his attention to one of the masks.

Who claims this mongrel?

Keith watched the Eagle spirit unfold itself, float down from its perch and circle counterclockwise slowly around the chamber. Its feathered wings rose and fell in the thick air. The beads and sticks sewn into its robes clattered to a slow ancient rhythm.

He is not one of us. At this, his eyes caught movement to one side. He turned and saw the Snake slither rapidly, almost to him, then swerve to follow the Eagle. Keith's eyes jumped from mask to mask as, one by one, the spirits projected their thoughts into his head and leapt onto the bare earth to follow the Eagle.

He is of our blood, said Coyote.

Only part of his blood, Squirrel reminded them.

Enough to make a warrior? asked Bear.

Keith shivered. He didn't like being the center of this discussion.

If the heart is strong, the blood-line does not matter, Cougar said in strong voice.

We have seen little strength, **noted** Hawk.

He ran from trouble, Snake added.

Another time he stood fast, countered Badger.

The assembled spirits circled and danced over Keith. He felt apprehension weaken his bowels. Did they know everything about him? *What should I be doing?* His head reeled from trying to follow the voice of each new creature that spoke.

It is early to judge, Eagle told the others. *His time still lies between child and man. His choice waits ahead on the path.*

Why is he here? asked Hawk.

Does he ask for help? wondered Squirrel.

He seeks council, Coyote said.

He is not fit, scoffed Snake.

A shaman brought him, noted Badger.

We will test him in battle against a strong adversary, Bear growled.

The battle is with himself, said Eagle, knowingly.

Keith realized something was missing. He pulled his eyes from the circling creatures and peered around the chamber. He twisted to look directly behind and saw the Wolf spirit shake itself as if to dry its long, thick fur; leap from its throne and fall in step with the Eagle.

I know him, Wolf said to Eagle.

Do you believe him to be worthy? asked Eagle.

I have seen into his heart. Watched him in a brave struggle. Felt his great loss.

Keith huddled beside the fire, transfixed by the Wolf's words, awed by the spectacle of painted phantoms, feathers, fur and jeweled robes whirling around him with their rhythmic clatter of accoutrements.

I will show him the Right Way, Wolf announced.

What will you demand in return? Eagle knew Wolf would extract a price for his counsel.

As if on command, the dancers pivoted in the air and landed in unison with a single crescendo of sound. In the abrupt silence, Keith felt the terrible gaze of all nine spirits penetrate him, grip his insides and squeeze until he could barely breathe. He grimaced, closed his eyes and then a rustling broke the quiet. The noise of shaken robes grew loud. When the rhythmic click of trinkets and bones reached a predetermined volume, the spirits, as one, released him. He opened his eyes and saw they had resumed the circling dance.

Others of his blood walk beside him, Cougar suggested.

Let it be one of them, Wolf said with finality.

All at once the nine specters halted again, landing with a single clap. Then came a cacophony of angry growls and hideous shrieks, a vision of slathering fangs and cruel beaks, not of masks, but of raging animals. Keith froze at the terrifying spectacle and thought he would pass out. The chamber darkened. All he could see was a circle of burning eyes surrounding him and then he was lost, floating in a dizzy emptiness. He lost track of time. Eventually, his vision returned and he was standing alone on top of a wide butte, surrounded by scrub and scattered pines. His legs felt unsteady. Bright light forced him to squint and he could just make out a dull rocky plain below stretching to a flat horizon in every direction. From a clear sky, a noonday sun burned his skin. In the still air, sweat leaked from his armpits, rolled beneath his shirt.

He took a step, but froze at a sudden whir in the brush. He snapped toward the sound and saw the Snake spirit zigzagging over the ground, a dark streak racing toward him. On reflex, Keith jumped six feet backwards. He tore off his shirt and waved it in his left hand. The Snake went for the shirt. Keith lunged for the Snake. His right hand reached for a spot behind the head. When he grabbed it, the Snake vanished in a mist of blue powder. Caught off balance, Keith fell on his side. Confused, he shook his head, looked at the blue powder on his hand and then up into the yellow eyes of the Wolf standing just beyond his reach.

You're not helpless. The silent message sounded inside his head. *What will you do with Hawk?*

Keith had barely understood the question when a shrill screech pierced his ears, thumping wings beat his face and burning pain ravaged his left shoulder. He rolled left and swatted at the raptor with his right hand. The Hawk withdrew its talons, flapped a few feet higher and then dropping like a stone, this time sinking its hooks into the boy's chest.

Keith shouted at the sudden pain and flailed both arms at the attacking Hawk, but it refused to release him. In desperation he rolled over, intending to trap the bird beneath him. Just when he thought he'd succeed, the creature vaporized in a puff of blue powder. Keith raised his head and once again encountered the yellow eyes of the Wolf.

Not so good, said the voice inside his head.

Keith regarded the canine and warily rose to his feet. He looked down at his chest. Touched the wounds. Grimaced. Panted.

What does Hawk want?

He searched the Wolf's eyes for the source of the question and was surprised to find sympathy.

To protect its young, fallen to the ground.

Keith searched around his feet and spotted two chicks huddled in the sand.

All creatures follow a path. Know their journey as you know your own. Avoid harm to their spirits, as do all creatures.

A loud roar drew Keith's eyes to the far edge of the butte. A black bear balanced on its hind legs, its head and neck weaving back and forth, its eyes locked on Keith.

Fear is now your enemy. Make it your friend.

Keith's eyes bulged. Fear in climbing, yes, but facing a wild and unpredictable carnivore?

He is not unpredictable. Is he hungry? Do you threaten him? Learn, what does Bear want?

The Bear dropped to all fours began to approach. *What does he want?* Keith needed tremendous willpower to take his eyes off the animal even for a second and search the surrounding sage for clues. Nothing. The Bear came on. Keith looked into the sparse pines. Still nothing. The Bear stood again, roared and wagged its head. The creature was forty feet away. It dropped to all fours and began running toward him. Keith spun around, took one step, and instantly realized running was the wrong answer. At that moment he sensed a light mist surround him and he caught a whiff of beeswax and honey. Instantly, he saw the bees hovering around the crook of a pine just ahead. He sprinted for the tree. Heard the charging bear closing the distance. A wave of blind terror clouded his head, paralyzed his spine; yet, he lunged at the forked branches and knocked the hive to the ground. Bent over and stumbling, he managed to cup the rolling hive in one hand and launch it backward into the path of the oncoming Bear before falling forward into the sage.

The visage of the Wolf not longer surprised Keith. The Bear had disappeared. He stood again but this time the Wolf seemed even larger.

Against Cougar, you cannot win a fight or run faster.

Keith tried to catch his breath. He leaned forward with his palms on his knees, wheezed, and continued to stare at the ground. He realized that his legs were shaking.

Did you not fly before?

He looked up into the Wolf's eyes. "Yes, but this is a dream. In my world, I don't fly."

Have courage. Your dreams have wisdom.

"Or nonsense."

Yes. But that is why you study. So you can choose wisely when you must.

Keith straightened up. Behind him was the edge of the butte. In front, the Cougar a dozen feet away. The Cougar charged. Keith spun. He dug in his toes hard and leapt into space. He was in the smoke again, suspended over the chasm, looking down into Suzanne's terrified eyes. Her piercing scream woke him with a start.

Somoma sat beside him on the woven rug, their mugs in front of him. The Shaman's legs were crossed and his expression was peaceful. He opened his eyes and looked at Keith. "It was an instructive trip?"

"I saw the Wolf."

Somoma's gaze sharpened.

"There were other animals. At least I think they were animals."

Somoma reflected for a moment. "You are young, but you have an old spirit."

"It happened fast. I didn't understand everything," he heard his own disappointment.

"You should have stayed longer."

"I didn't mean to wake up."

The Shaman looked at him with kind eyes. "The dream terrified you. It takes courage to remain there."

"The Wolf talked about courage."

"It is how men become warriors."

"I went to a terrible place."

"Yes, the place of fear. We must all journey through it."

"I wasn't afraid," he protested.

"You didn't recognize fear." The Shaman smiled. "But you returned quickly to this room."

"What about my friend?"

"You dreamed of your sister."

Keith shivered. "I know."

"Her death troubles you more than your friend."

"I thought I would see him."

"The answer we get...you know...is not always the one we sought."

"How will I—"

Somoma cut him off. "Let your spirit help you find the answer." Then he regarded the artwork anew. "Meanwhile, I will study this painting harder. Perhaps the white man who painted it did see a wolf."

~

I hope he doesn't offer coffee, Winston thought as he followed Parker's secretary into the office. *It's too close to lunch and my stomach is killing me.* Out of the corner of his eye, he saw Rusty outline her hourglass shape with his hands. He slid a frown at the deputy then turned to greet Parker, but was immediately distracted by the menagerie of mounted animals cluttering the office. The gyrfalcon shifted on its perched in the far side of the room and speared him with a fierce predatory stare. He froze. Rusty froze. Parker, apparently, was used to this reaction. "Prizes retrieved by my cast of falcons," he said as he came around the desk to greet them. "And that's Merlin. Pay him no mind." Winston shook Davis' hand and was followed by Deputy Rodriguez. "Sheriff, deputy. Come in. Sit down."

They dropped into two chairs before the desk while Parker went behind it. Rusty sat closest to the gyrfalcon, uncomfortably near the cold threat of its gleaming eyes.

Once ensconced in his Aeron throne, Parker came right to the point. "Something about Hayden, you said."

"We're just being thorough, Mr. Davis," Winston replied. "Checking out everyone who knew Tito Montoya."

Parker scowled. "That was an ugly thing. I feel for Manny. He's one of the lab's best construction supervisors."

The sheriff paused for a second, then asked, "What can you tell us about Mr. Carlysle's actions yesterday afternoon?"

"He was at work in his office on an important project that's due tomorrow."

"Anyone see him?"

Parker stopped to think. "His secretary saw him go into his office right after lunch and stay there until she left at five."

"Did she see him during that time?"

"No. He asked not to be disturbed."

"How did she know he was there?" Winston didn't hesitate.

"There's nowhere else he could go without her seeing him leave." Parker said, as if it was obvious.

"Yes, but how do we know he was really there? How do we know he didn't climb out the window or something?"

Parker smiled at him. "Sheriff. C'mon. That's not Hayden."

"Sorry, but we have to cover all our bases."

Winston watched Parker pause and appeared to search for corroboration before continuing. "Security maintains a keystroke log for every terminal used in classified work at the lab. Hayden's office computer is one of those. The logs confirm that his terminal was in use all afternoon."

"Isn't it possible to fool the system?" Winston asked.

Parker produced an incredulous look. "Boy, you are a suspicious one."

"A boy's been murdered."

Parker rolled the suggestion around in his head. "In theory, yes, it's possible. But it would be extremely time consuming and difficult."

"But it *is* possible?"

"Sheriff," Parker's tone indicated that his patience was running thin. "You know Hayden. He is an exceptional scientist. He's worked here since college. His behavior has always been exemplary. He's not someone who would commit murder."

"You're probably right, Mr. Davis. But, as I said, we're just being thorough."

Parker stood, indicating the interview was finished. Winston rose and saw that the gyrfalcon had entranced his deputy.

"That is a beautiful bird, Mr. Davis," Rusty said.

"Merlin is a gyrfalcon, deputy. Prized by kings and noblemen for centuries. You ought to see him hunt sometime."

"Wow. I heard you guys did falconry up here——"

Winston cut off the banter. "Deputy Rodriguez! We gotta go. The man's busy."

"That's okay, sheriff. I like people who can appreciate savage beauty."

~

Hayden moved aimlessly around the garage, stopping occasionally to grab a mug from the workbench and sip stale morning coffee. He picked up a valve cover that lay beside the cup. Last week he'd started machining it for the Ducati in the empty parking bay. He examined the metal, ran his fingers over the rough edges, looked at the motorcycle's disassembled engine, the dishpan of motor oil underneath, and decided he wasn't up for it today. The cover went back beside the coffee. Hayden paced, rubbed his palms on his jeans, stopped, and stared at a photo of Suzanne. She smiled at him from a sunny day beside a lake, happy, innocent, hopeful.

Hayden wanted more than anything to explain himself, *I couldn't let him get away with it. He destroyed your life and I destroyed his.*

He flicked the tears away. The workbench, the cup, the valve cover, the shop returned to focus. Hayden steadied himself, caught his breath. He found a rag and blew his nose. He was sweating. He grabbed the phone and, dialed. It was answered on the second ring, "Uplink. Major Grey speaking."

"Elliot. This is Hayden Carlysle."

"Carlysle. Good grief, I was wondering how you were."

"I've been thinking over the issue with NANCY. I'd like to discuss a revision. Wondered if you're around this afternoon?"

"Yes, indeed. I will be in my office, Carlysle, but no, unfortunately, I cannot invite you to join me."

"What do you mean?"

"The general has instructed me to suspend contact until your daughter's incident is resolved."

"What?"

"Yes, sir. It seems you are officially a security risk."

"Jesus. What am I supposed to do about NANCY?"

"I don't know. My guess would be to talk to Parker."

Hayden contemplated the photograph, shook his head. "Hard to fathom the mind of HQ, Elliot. I'll get back to you."

"Thanks for understanding, Carlysle. Good luck."

~

Hayden burst through the door of Parker's office and found him standing with the white gyrfalcon on his glove, stroking its head. He spoke without thinking. "Grey says he can't talk to me until my incident is resolved. What am I supposed to do? Our deadline's tomorrow!"

Parker was on top of it. "Security, Jesus. They should have cleared that from their book by now. I'll talk to them. Can you get along or do you need to talk with him?"

"I need to talk to him. We've got to reach a decision on discrimination."

"I'll take care of it," Parker swung one leg over the edge of his desk and scrutinized Hayden. "You heard about Manny's kid?"

Hayden lowered his eyes and nodded. "I saw Manny last night."

"Another god damn tragedy." Parker stood and carried Merlin to his stand. "The Army's imagery any help?"

"It was tough to tell."

"Yeah, Grey said it was ambiguous, but intriguing."

Hayden frowned.

"So, how are you doing?" Parker asked him.

"Oh fine," Hayden's sarcasm was transparent. "My daughter falls off a cliff and no one knows why. We've got a deadline tomorrow and security has tied my hands. Doesn't that sound just fine to you?"

Parker was sympathetic. "Anything I can do to help?"

"I wish there was." Hayden calmed himself.

Parker eased Merlin onto the perch and removed his leather gauntlet. "Sheriff was here. Asked about you."

"Doing his job I suppose."

"That's what he said."

Hayden lowered his head, couldn't look Parker in the eye. *I must tell him*, he thought, but when he spoke, the words come out low and scratchy. "I need to say something about my work on the NANCY project."

Parker took the chair behind his desk and assumed the role of Hayden's superior. "Yes, the major says you may reconfigure NANCY, give the Army more leeway with collateral damage. That true?"

Hayden realized that his friend was now his boss. "It was a suggestion, yes."

Parker bristled. "NANCY is supposed to save innocent lives and thereby protect the Army."

"She is."

"Why the change?"

"Elliot—Major Grey—thinks her rules are too strict."

"Zero tolerance, you said. Only way to keep 'em honest."

"I'm not sure anymore." He didn't like Parker's direction.

Parker leaned forward on his desk. "The ethical constructs you created for NANCY are her strength. Are you going to abandoning them this late in the program?"

Hayden put his hands on his hips. "They may not be right. She makes decisions on cold facts. Now, I think she needs emotion" He looked at Parker with conviction. "Otherwise, there's no justice?"

Parker snorted. "Don't go flip-flopping on us, Hayden. NANCY has performed brilliantly. No one else can teach her to determine whether a satellite image is gonna shoot a gun."

"I know that, but now Army wants her to—"

Parker cut him off. "Stop right there. NANCY's rules are not up to one major, or even one general. We have a go-ahead because the folks higher up know she will save lives, change the way we fight wars. We've got to deliver on that promise. Now, I don't care how you do it, but you have until tomorrow to finalize her algorithms."

Hayden glared at his boss. "Parker, you're pushing me."

"I am." Parker stretched across the desk. "And I will continue to push you until we deliver NANCY."

"I need an answer from Major Grey."

"You'll have it!"

Hayden wasn't used to rejection. NANCY was, after all, his concept, his program and people, generally, had been content to follow his lead. He stepped backward, looked away, and thought, *What am I supposed to be working on?* The multidimensional road map, normally etched so clearly in his mind, the one that allowed him to visualize the intricate logic and subroutines of NANCY's programming, was suddenly a torn and faded parchment of unrelated artifacts. He looked at Parker with a blank stare.

"You okay, Hayden?

He turned slowly and stepped toward door. "I'll let you know."

~

Hayden returned home in the afternoon, left the Audi in the driveway and entered the living room through the front door. He was on his way into the kitchen, but stopped in the doorway when he heard Keith and Lucy deep in discussion. He stood unnoticed. Keith sat at the kitchen table. Lucy carried lunch dishes to the sink.

"Mom, it was like a dream only real," Keith said, his voice full of amazement.

"Did you see your spirit?"

"I saw a Wolf."

Lucy smiled with pride, "Ah, the Teacher we say. Listen to him, my son, and learn much. Learn who you are. How to be strong, balance your life. When to fight, when to speak."

"Really? All this time, I thought he was just a symbol of freedom."

She turned to Keith. "Only if he was alone when you saw him." She noticed Hayden, sent him a hello glance, and looked back at Keith. "What else?"

"I—I woke up. Somoma said it was because I was afraid."

"Were you?"

"No," he sounded defensive.

Hayden moved into the room toward Lucy and watched Keith wrestle over whether to say more. "Mom. I need to tell you something about what happened. It's really important—"

He stepped into Keith's view and snapped at him. "What's important? A fantasy trip to the spirit world?"

"Hayden!" Lucy was shocked. "What's the matter with you? Keith's done nothing wrong."

Hayden stared down at his son, his sarcasm growing to full outrage. "Of course not. Nobody's done anything wrong. Our daughter falls off a cliff. No one knows anything. I've got a project deadline tomorrow. I can't talk to the Army liaison. We're not going to deliver on time. Innocents will die. I'm going to lose my job. No, there's nothing wrong here!"

Keith had never heard intense frustration from his father. He turned to face him and in return received a sour look. "You disappoint me," Hayden said to him. "Your sister's dead and what are you doing about it?"

Keith froze for about two seconds before his face reddened. He flung back the chair and stood to confront his father. "Just what am I supposed to do, Dad?" Before Hayden could respond, Keith pushed Hayden angrily aside and ran for the door. Hayden tripped and fell backward. His head hit the tile floor and he didn't hear the kitchen door slam after his son.

"Keith! Come back here." Lucy's words fell unheard. She glared down at Hayden. "Get control of yourself, will you? Look what you've done. You're both losing it."

Hayden lay motionless, his glazed eyes locked on the ceiling. From the left side of his head, a pool of hot blood spread over cold tile.

~

When he awoke, Hayden was surprised to find himself in bed. He was shocked by the pain in his head until he recalled falling. He reached up and felt gauze wrapping that blocked part of his vision and knew he had been unconscious for a while. He lay face up under the bed covers.

He heard Lucy enter from the bathroom, peeked over, and saw her rubbing crème on her face. Her eyes studied him like a sick child as she circled the bed and sat beside him. She placed both hands on his chest and tried to move into his field of view. "You believe you've lost your way. Am I right?"

He took a deep breath and shut his eyes.

"Because of Suzanne?"

At the sound of her name, he grimaced and turned his head away.

"I haven't been much help. Have I?"

He lay still for several seconds before turning to her with anguish in his eyes and frustration in his voice.

"The innocent life of a child. Did I do the right thing?"

He felt her hands press into him and her tone grow stern.

"That's the problem, Hayden. You haven't done anything. You look dead. Snap out of it. I'm just as sorry about Suzanne as you are. But Keith and I need you. Help us move on. Don't hurt us. Please?"

He felt unheard. She couldn't answer his real question, *Did I do the right think killing Keith?* because she didn't know he'd done it. He closed his eyes and turned away.

Lucy withdrew her hands from his chest and stood slowly. "This is not like you."

~

Winston watched headlights in the twilight pan across the lawn outside his office window and hoped for an easy night. *A quiet night, please. We've got lots of work to do. No interruptions.*

Having established his frame of mind, he spun the chair from the dark window into the bright office. Rusty had just grabbed the only other chair. The two officers, Anderson and Martini, knew the pecking order and were leaning against the file cabinets.

Winston sat forward, jabbed his elbows on the desk. He turned his head purposefully to his right hand and watched his fingers twirl a carved wolf amulet. Without looking away he said, "Martini. How did you and four deputies miss finding this during the initial search?"

"It wasn't on the ground, chief. It was caught on a piece of sagebrush."

He glanced at the officer. "Yeah, almost on top of where the body landed."

Martini looked at the floor. His voice got quiet. "I know, chief. I'm sorry."

"Do I have to send you guys to the optometrist?"

"No, chief," Martini mumbled again.

"Well, when are you gonna learn to be more thorough? Every hour that goes by without a break cuts our chances of solving the case. The trail grows cold. Then what?"

"With all respect, chief, we're not used to these kinds of crimes around here," Anderson chimed in.

"Well, that's for sure." He faced the other officer. "Your inexperience probably cost us a day and a half."

Martini and Anderson exchanged looks of shame.

Winston softened his frown."The good news is you found it. I think we now know Tito's killer."

Even though he looked confidently at the three deputies, none of them registered any joy at the news.

~

Keith hoped to make it into his room without alerting his parents. With luck they would be in bed. He stole along the upstairs hallway with shoes in hand. When he finally entered his bedroom, he left the door ajar, like he always did, sat on his bed, and relaxed. Safe. After a moment, he silently changed into pajamas and got into bed.

He lay there thinking about his father when he heard the phone ring. His mother's slippers scuffled hurriedly down the hall, down the stairs and her hand lifted the receiver from the hook after the fourth ring. Her voice sounded firm, like she was right outside his doorway.

"Hello," she said.

Pause

"Oh, Tom. Hi. That's okay, you didn't disturb us.

Pause

"No. I haven't seen Keith this evening."

Pause

At the sound of his name, he threw off the covers and sneaked to the doorway.

"Do you want me to give him a message?"

Pause

"I do expect him. Shall I have him call you?"

Keith ran a hand through his hair, worried.

"Oh. Well. Does he know what it's about?"

He didn't wait to hear more. He took his clothes from the chair and began to dress. From downstairs, his mother said, "All right, Tom. I'll have him do that."

Keith skulked again, shoes in hand, out of his room and down the hall, out the back, the same way he had arrived.

~

The spicy smell of burnt piñon lingered in Manny's den year round. The fireplace enhanced the warmth and feel of the small room's knotty pine walls, woven Indian carpets and comfortable leather lounge chairs. His visit to the Carlysle home hadn't improved his spirits and he felt that escaping into the cradle of his favorite TV chair, a cold beer, and the mindlessness replays of the day's baseball games, would get his mind off of Tito.

The sound of his wife's footsteps trampled his reverie. He glanced up—long enough to see that Rachel wore a jacket and carried her purse—and looked back at the screen.

"Where you been?"

"Work. Just like every day."

"I'll bet."

"You'll never guess what I heard."

"No, I won't."

Rachael twirled and made for the door. "Okay. You don't want to know the latest on our son."

Manny slammed his chair upright and faced her. The sound froze Rachael in her tracks. "What the fuck you talking about?"

She turned, saw the menace in his eyes and backed against the wall. "We heard at the store that Tom Winston is looking all over for Keith Carlysle."

"Keith?" The news confused him. He rose from the chair as if to do something, but once on his feet, he paused. "Boy, I got that one wrong."

"Whaddya mean?" Rachael pressed into the wall.

Manny didn't respond, just stood and contemplated. After a moment, he crossed the room to the gun cabinet next to the TV and pulled open the door.

"What are you thinking?" Rachael sobbed.

Manny grabbed a holstered revolver from the case, turned, and placed it on the table between them. Guns always made her nervous. He stared at her and watched her eyes widen with fear.

"Manny!"

His lips flattened in a cruel smile. He unbuckled his leather belt, slipped on the holster. "I gotta talk with that boy."

"What are you going to do?"

Manny strode blindly past Rachael on his way out of the room. "Gotta find him. Wanna talk."

"Where are you going?"

Manny kept walking, didn't turn or look around. "Burnt Mesa, where those kids always go."

Rachael remained glued to the wall until she heard Manny's truck start. Then her body went slack and she stepped away from the wall. She took the nearest chair and reached for the telephone, then thought better of it and went into the living room and sat on the couch.

~

To a woman, Sanrio's trailer announced that he lived like a slob. To a man, it said this guy was busy. He lived in his shop. What's wrong with that?

The trailer had a kitchen, but its only functioning parts were a grimy sink, for washing hands; the stove's left rear burner, for heating coffee; and a small refrigerator, to hold beer and trays of small mechanical parts. The greenish linoleum had been swept once and then covered with small engines, generators, carburetors, a post hole digger, chain saws of every size, blenders, toasters, broilers, vacuum cleaners, waffle irons, clothes irons, mechanical and electronic calculators, radios, and TVs. Every item bore a blue tag with a name and date. Every counter surface supported racks of narrow drawers filled with spare parts, all sorted and labeled.

The only disorganized place was the Formica table where Sanrio sat reassembling a chain saw amidst a forest of empty beer cans and fast food wrappers. *Fucking Ortega*, he thought, *never remembers the oil. What does he expect? Next time, I'm charging him double.*

A dirt-encrusted Bakelite phone under a Burger King wrapper rang with the authority of the bell in a prison yard. Sanrio snatched the receiver with one hand, snapped it into the crook of his shoulder, and clinched it to his ear. His other hand continued working on the saw.

"Yeah," he said without care. As he listened, his hands lowered slowly to the table, he released the tools and shifted his entire attention to the phone.

"Chica! Chica! Slow down. Say it again so I can understand."

With the phone in one hand, he leaned the chair back on two legs, opened the refrigerator door, and grabbed a can of beer.

"No shit?" he said into the phone. "He's after the brother?"

He let the chair fall forward and popped open the beer. Her words astonished him.

"Oh yeah? What's the *maricón* gonna do?"

His incredulity soared. "He took a gun?" Sanrio stood and walked into the bedroom dragging thirty-feet of extension cord with the phone still to his ear. His eyes glowed as he listened.

"Chica, this is perfect."

~

On the other end of the line, Rachael held the phone, tears staining her cheeks, brooding. "Listen, Machuque. I'm not sure."

She listened to him while her eyes surveyed the room, the artifacts of her marriage: family photos, a wedding mantilla, bronzed baby shoes. Then she responded, "Yeah, but I keep thinking things aren't so bad like they are. Let's not mess it up."

She spun the wedding ring on her left hand.

"Please, Machuque. I'm begging you. Don't do this now."

~

In the bedroom of his trailer, Sanrio reached into the open closet and fetched a revolver in a holster from the shelf above the hanging clothes.

"Chica, no. We couldn't ask for a better opportunity. Do you know where he went?"

He clenched the phone to his ear and slipped the holster onto his belt. "Yeah, I know it. Above Frijoles Canyon." He drew the gun, inspected the cylinder, saw it was loaded.

"Chica. I want you to go to Sheila's now. Stay there 'til you hear from me."

He returned the gun to its holster. "Right. So someone knows where you are. And don't worry. I'll call you *muy pronto*. Okay, bye."

Sanrio hung up the phone. His face broke into grin and he punched the air three times. "Yes. Yes. Yes."

He snatched his hat and plowed out the door. "You're my *puta* now, motherfucker."

~

Hayden couldn't sleep. He came downstairs and laid on the living room couch watching flames dance in the fireplace. He unwrapped the bandage from his head and the one from his left hand to study the wound. He extended his arm, flexed the fingers, and groaned. *Not ready,* he thought. He rewrapped the hand and fell back to catch his breath.

Lucy marched into the room and over to the couch, pushed his body aside to make a space, and sat. "Hayden, I'm worried. Tom Winston called looking for Keith. I said we hadn't seen him. But I just went to his room. He's been and gone."

His looked up. "What's it about?"

"Tito. Half the town must know Tom's looking for Keith. If the Montoya family thinks he had something to do with Tito, they might —"

Hayden watched Lucy as he massaged his hand.

She looked desperate. "I can't go through this again. He's all we've got."

Hayden continued to study his wife and felt his own anxiety grow. "Lucy, I've got to say this. For two days I've been fighting myself to get this out: I am responsible for Tito's death."

She was stunned. "You?"

"Me. I wasn't sure until I saw satellite images. He pushed Suzanne off the edge of Burnt Mesa into Frijoles Canyon."

She looked at him with her mouth agape.

"I saw him in the park after she fell. In the jail, I heard him yell how he hurt her, how she got what she deserved. He told me he saw her on Burnt Mesa. Then, there's the satellite—"

"So you killed him?"

"He killed Suzanne. He deserved it."

Her face contorted with anger and sadness, she balled up her fists and held them in front of her. Her voice was hollow. "My God, Hayden. What have you done?"

"What I had to. Tom just let him go."

"I cannot believe that you thought killing a boy was all right."

"Not a boy, a predator. He used her and then pushed her off a cliff. I watched her fall. He broke my heart. Broke your heart."

Lucy looked at Hayden and he saw that his words had broken her beyond repair. Her eyes were glassy, her voice full of despair. She wailed, "And now what? People blame Keith. They're after him, not you."

Hayden sat up with a start. "Damn!" He looked at Lucy. "Manny. From last night, I know what he's thinking."

He fumbled his feet into his shoes. Then he stood and headed to the kitchen. Her shout stopped him.

"Have you forgotten the value of life, Hayden?"

He looked back at her. "I know what our daughter's life meant to us, if that's what you mean."

"And if Keith gets hurt, you'll find out again." She slowed for emphasis. "Only it will be too late."

He continued into the kitchen. His wife's words followed him through quiet house, *My God, Hayden. What have you done?*

He opened the door into the back yard. The cool air blew refreshingly on his skin. The cedars looked clean and crisp in the silver moonlight. He made himself breathe deeply and was overwhelmed. *What the hell have I done?*

A moving shadow caught his eye as it arched over the split-rail fence on his right: a flash of grey—a wolf streaking across the bright yard toward his left—bounding at a dead run, leaping the far fence, and disappearing.

Hayden stood perplexed. What had he just seen? It took a moment for his mind to catch up to his eyes. He couldn't explain why, but he suddenly felt energized, purposeful. He closed the door and returned to the living room. Lucy was still on the couch, head in her hands. He touched her hair. "I'm going to help Keith."

She looked up. Her face was puffy. "Can you find him?"

"I have a good idea where he is." He hurried to the front door.

~

Rusty's voice broke through the static of the police radio and filled Winston's cruiser. "Tom, my twenty is the Reel Deal."

Winston keyed the radio on his shoulder. "Rusty, I don't think he went to the movies. Do you think you could try McDonalds?"

"Sure, boss," came the reply. "I just wanted to check with the cashier—"

Winston keyed the radio several times to interrupt his deputy. "Rusty, for crying out loud, leave that girl alone and get on with it. We need to find the kid soon. Before someone else does." The radio stayed silent for a long moment before Winston heard, "Ten-four."

He drove slowly past the high school, eyed a few pedestrians, a few drivers, and then steered for the north side of town. Nothing. He pulled off the road onto the tarmac in front of Juan's Shop 'n Drop, found a parking spot at the end of a row of cars and shut of the engine. A group of teenage boys lolled in the harsh fluorescent glare by the entrance. *How can they think they look attractive?* Tom thought and exited the car.

They recognized Keith in the photograph, but no one had seen him. Nor had the clerk inside or the group of girls reading magazines and giggling by the front window. He strode back to the cruiser and decided to head into the center of town and join Rusty.

~

Manny drove the Chevy pickup like a drunken madman through the outskirts of Los Alamos, squealing around corners, barely missing parked cars. "I know where you are hiding, motherfucker," he growled and accelerated into a blind curve on the two-lane road to Bandelier.

He wiped the sweat from his eyes with his right wrist and looked out the windshield just in time to see the turnoff for the dirt track that lead to Burnt Mesa. He spun the wheel and watched the headlights bounce around the turn onto the shortcut. The rutted trail disappeared in the scrub ahead. The truck rocked dangerously as it followed the headlights around an s-turn. The beams rose over sharp rocky rise and dipped unexpectedly into an arroyo.

He goosed the engine to shoot out of the ditch, but felt the truck drift to the left and slow to a stop. The tires spun in the sand. "Shit," he cursed and revved the engine repeatedly, but felt the wheels dig deeper into the dirt. *Well, that's that,* he thought and killed the engine.

Manny leapt out of the pickup. His boots landed in sand. He slammed the door, kicked the truck, and gave an exasperated snort. He glowered at the truck for a long time, his breaths short and shallow. Then he began to sway back and forth on his feet and suddenly remembered his mission. He drew the revolver, checked the cylinder, and re-holstered. Without even a glance around, he scrambled up the embankment, leaving a wide trail in the smooth sand. It was clearly visible in the headlights he neglected to switch off. At the top of the rise, he ducked into the scrub and disappeared.

~

When Hayden turned the Audi onto the two-lane road for Burnt Mesa, he saw a slight haze of dust linger over the rutted groves. He worried that Manny was ahead of him and stepped on the accelerator. The station wagon sped through the s-curves, dipped into the arroyo, and suddenly encountered Manny's truck sunk deep in the sand on the left side of the road. He skidded to a stop. The Chevy's headlights shown on the embankment, but Hayden saw no one around. He reached under the seat for a flashlight and stepped cautiously out of the Audi.

He shined a light into the pickup cab and into the bed, but found nothing. He turned in a circle looking for clues and saw the swath of foot marks going up the embankment. He doused the flashlight, chased the footsteps out of the ditch, and sprinted through the scrub toward the canyon.

~

Running in moonlight through the wilderness was a joy Sanrio had treasured since childhood. It was freedom, the right of all Indians. Now his feet fell silently on a footpath that meandered through the piñon and sage on Burnt Mesa. His face showed no strain in spite of the fast pace. He was gliding through the twists and dips of a dry creek bed.

He emerged from the thick brush and found himself again on the flat mesa. He had traveled thirty yards when an unfamiliar presence seemed to coalesce in his body. His face grew attentive. He cocked his head to one side.

Did I hear something? No. Besides, whatever it is won't catch me. Keep running.

Yet, the shadow within him persisted, forced him to listen again.

I hear breathing. No, panting. Something trying to catch me? Just a quick glance back. Nothing. Keep running.

The heavy breaths sounded closer. Without thinking, he ran faster. Another glance back. No fear, just puzzlement. When he turned again to the trail in front, he saw a tree in the path and dogged left to avoid it. As he came around the trunk and back onto the path, he didn't immediately see the glowering yellow eyes and savage jowls. Or hear the menacing growl. But his lightening reflexes stopped him as though he'd hit a wall. Only then did he see the wolf, ferocious, barring his trail. Sanrio was trapped. And hypnotized. His eyes locked on the terrible jaws, the long vicious canines.

The monster was fierce. It threatened, lurched forward. Instinctively, Sanrio stilled his body, dropped his eyes to the ground. His peripheral vision caught the snap of its bared teeth and his ears heard the growls threatening in the animal's throat.

I am a statue.

The demon darted in with a vicious slash.

Don't move. Don't look in its eyes. My hand will creep slowly, stealthily, imperceptibly up to the holster on my belt. No? It can sense my purpose?

Sanrio heard the deep snarl. Felt the impact of its lunge. The weight pushed him on his back and he saw a wicked snap of jaws near his chest. The grey beast vaulted over his head. He swung around in time to see it lope up the trail, throw back its head, and send a chilling howl into the night.

He drew the revolver, rolled to his stomach, up on his elbows. He aimed, but the fiend disappeared before he could fire. Dropping his hands, he rolled to his side and let his fingers probe the gaping, bloody wound on his chest.

~

Keith sat close to the fire, arms clasped around his upraised knees, chin resting on his forearms. His eyes contemplated an eerie panorama: the dark and deadly canyon in front of him, the sinister mesa to either side, its rocks and vegetation cast into stark relief by the full moon. The only sound in the still air was the crackle from the fire in its shallow pit. The only smell was burning piñon.

He longed for his sister, his companion from before he could remember. He asked himself repeatedly, *Why had she been so stupid. Fucking Tito then letting him mess her up. If only I could have saved her.*

A baleful sound broke his reverie. A long wolf howl floated ominously over the canyon. It transported him back to his awakening dream, the one Somoma had said frightened him. He recalled the smoky image of the dream wolf and shivered.

A scuffling, in the brush, drew his attention to the trail behind him. He turned his head, looked over his left shoulder and was startled to see an irate man bearing down on him in the firelight. He jumped to his feet and put the fire between himself and the intruder with his face contorted in rage and streaked with dirt, his clothes torn and stained. Keith's brain strained to identify the wrathful features. They suddenly resolved and he shouted, "Mr. Montoya?"

Manny lumbered closer, his eyes ablaze. "Now I've gotcha, you murdering little shit."

Keith stepped back. "Mr. Montoya, please. What's the matter?"

Manny kept coming. "You killed my son."

Keith retreated another step. "What? No, you're wrong. I didn't."

The words had no effect. Manny drew a revolver and aimed straight at him. "That's not what the sheriff says."

"Why would I?" Keith's voice rose an octave. "Tito was my friend."

"You thought he killed Suzanne."

"No, I didn't."

Manny shook the pistol at him. "Don't lie to me, boy."

Someone yelled Manny's name from the direction of the highway. Keith looked past the fire, past Manny, toward the sound, and glimpsed Manny turning also. His father came to a stop past Manny, out of breath. Hayden bent at the waist, supported himself with the right hand on one knee and raised his bandaged left.

"Wait," his father said.

Keith shifted focus to Manny, who faced Hayden, but couldn't decide where to point his weapon. When Keith started around the fire toward Hayden, Manny pointed the gun at him again.

"Don't move. You're not going anywhere. You murdered my son."

Hayden managed to stand upright. He lowered his hand, looked at Manny and gasped. "Keith didn't kill Tito, Manny. I did."

Keith couldn't believe it. He heard Manny stammer, "Hayden. I...I...you swore—"

"I lied. It was me. Leave him alone."

Manny lowered the gun, dumbfounded. "You thought Tito killed Suzanne?"

"I heard him. He said he hurt her. Called her a tramp. Said she deserved it."

Keith was confused. Manny looked at him, just as confused, then turned back to Hayden, raised the gun and took aim. "Motherfucker. You're dead."

Keith felt his own panic. He swiveled his head and darted his eyes frantically around the circle of undergrowth lit by the fire. They caught the glow of yellow eyes in the sagebrush to his left. In a split second he heard their message as surely as if they had spoken.

Know their journey as well as you know your own.

He saw what he needed to do. Instantly, he bounded past the fire, past Manny, into the space between the two men, and shouted at his father in an unfamiliar guttural voice, "No, Dad. I was there! In the jail. Tito was talking about something else. He didn't kill Suzanne. He only hurt her." The boy's powerful surge caught them off guard.

Manny glared at him, "Tito wouldn't hurt Suzanne."

He turned to Manny with black contempt. "Suzanne told Tito she had sex with you. He got mad and punched her."

Hayden scowled at Manny, "You had sex with my daughter?"

Manny lowered the gun and looked down. "I—I, no, I didn't."

"Fuck you, Manny!" Keith shouted. "She said you fucked her in the front seat of your truck."

"No, man," he looked at Keith. "It wasn't like that. I mean—yeah something happened but it wasn't my fault." He turned to Hayden. "She came on to me. Begged me. I didn't know what to do. I was weak. I've been living in shame ever since. I feel so bad."

"She was fourteen, Manny," her father spit the words. "You're responsible no matter what she does. I thought you could be trusted."

Manny looked contrite. "It happened a long time ago."

"What?" Hayden demanded, his face reddening.

"Last year," he barely whispered.

"Thirteen. Jesus." Hayden's words made Keith turn. He saw his father gnash his bandaged fist into his good palm struggling to find the right action. He gritted his teeth and moved in a semicircle so they faced Manny together, side by side.

While Hayden brooded, Keith scowled at Manny and watched him wilt before his eyes. Then his father raised his clenched fists and bellowed at Manny, "You're to blame for this whole insane mess. You and Tito. For Suzanne's death—"

Keith interrupted. "No, Dad. Not Suzanne's death. She slipped, there, on the cliff. I tried to save her but she fell."

Hayden turned slowly. His jaw dropped and he stared at Keith. His hands fell to his sides. He stayed lost in thought for several moments. "The satellite." It came out low and scratchy.

"What?" Keith said.

"The images from the satellite. I saw them. There were two people on Burnt Mesa."

"Dad, what are you talking about?"

"I thought it was Tito," Hayden murmured. "It was you."

"Me and Suzanne?" Keith asked.

"Tito was innocent." The realization seemed to deflate Hayden who sank to his knees, brought his hands to his face, and shook his head.

No one moved for several seconds. Manny was first to comprehend the irony. "So, Keith was responsible for Suzanne's death, not Tito." He stalked over to Hayden, glared down at him, and spit the words. "All right, you smug, pig, hypocrite let me see you take retribution on your son like you did on mine."

Hayden kept his eyes on the ground, humbled. Keith wasn't sure what to expect. Then his father took a deep breath. With a determined look, he rose to his feet and came at him with a measured pace. Keith grew anxious. He didn't know what would happen. He held steadfast but felt his body sway. His father approached stone-faced. He felt his lips tremble. Hayden kept coming, his jaws clenched. At the last possible second Keith felt himself folded into a solid embrace, heard his father whisper into his ear. "I'm sorry, son. I must do this."

He didn't understand until Hayden turned to Manny, "Take my life, Manny. Tito was my fault."

Hayden released Keith and stepped away.

"Okay." Manny raised the weapon and aimed at Hayden.

Keith's mind was racing. *Control fear. Make it your friend.*

"Wait," Keith shouted and began to inch towards Manny. "Take me. Let him go."

Before Manny could reply Keith lunged. He felt, rather than saw, his father spring after him and with one hand push him out of the line of fire.

He felt the sudden concussion of the gun blast near his face, followed by the collision into Manny. He saw the gun fly from Manny's grasp as they crashed to the ground. He reached for Manny's arm and was startled by a hideous yell from the direction of the canyon. Keith turned and saw a bloody apparition stagger into the firelight. A tormented man held a revolver with both hands in front of his lacerated chest, aimed it at Manny, and raised his head to the moon. "You're my *puta* now you motherfucking *maricón* son of a bitch."

Manny was panic-stricken from the bloodlust in the Sanrio's glazed eyes. He rolled onto his belly and scrambled to get away. As Keith dove in the opposite direction, he heard two shots and raving laughter. He turned to look, saw Manny on his hands and knees, legs churning but going nowhere. Another shot. Manny grabbed his butt cheek and fell forward. Then he saw Hayden, who was laying on his back, snatch Manny's pistol from the ground beside him, roll to his side, and fire at the madman.

The bullet struck his throat and he collapsed sideways into a bloody heap. There was a horrific empty silence. No one breathed. Keith stared at the man with his head plunged into the dirt, one bloodshot eye staring back at him, watched his life drain into the sand, the eye cloud over.

He heard Manny groan and snapped back into the moment. He jumped to his feet, rushed to father and knelt beside him. "Dad?"

Hayden lay bleeding from a chest wound. Keith saw the spreading stain on his father's shirt and immediately looked for something to stop the blood. An instant later, he tore off his own shirt and pressed it to his father's chest.

Manny groaned again. Keith ignored him and concentrated on maintaining even pressure on the bandage. Hayden's eyes closed and desperation overcame Keith for several agonizing minutes before his father opened them again. Keith peered into his anguished face from inches away. Manny had crawled beside Keith and saw that Hayden had regained consciousness. He grabbed the boy's sleeve. "He's alive," he said, looking into Hayden's face. "You saved my life."

Hayden coughed, tried to speak, and coughed again before he was able to grunt, "Not yours. Keith's."

Manny squirmed either from pain or the knowledge that he was just the lucky benefactor of Hayden's action. But he was alive and thankful. "If it makes you feel better, I'm gonna think of you every day for the rest of my life, every time I take a shit."

~

Winston heard five pops as he and Rusty drove past the sand-trapped Chevy pickup with its lit headlights draining the battery, and around the Audi. He heard the shots and goosed the cruiser over the rough road. "Jesus, Rusty. I hope we get there in time."

As they approached the canyon rim, Rusty suddenly pointed out his window. "Look, chief. Over there. A fire." Winston saw the glow to his right a short way off the trail. He skidded to a stop and jumped out of the cruiser. He donned his hat, drew his 1911 .45 auto, and strode toward the glow in the trees with Rusty on his left shoulder. As they came close enough to see through the trees, Winston identified two men leaning over a third who lay on his back. He held his gun at the ready.

"Hello by the fire," he commanded. "This is the sheriff. No more shooting."

The two men on their knees turned at the sound of his voice.

"Okay, sheriff." He recognized Manny's voice. "Come along. No more shooting."

Winston and Rusty stepped into the circle of firelight and saw Manny and Keith beside Hayden. The Indian, Machuque, lay slumped on the ground a few feet away. Winston guessed by the position of the body that it was dead. He noted the location of the guns, one by Hayden, the other near Machuque. He looked at Manny and Keith. "Not a pretty sight." Then shook his head. "Rusty, grab those guns. Any more guns, boys?"

"No," said Manny. "Just those two."

"Anyone else hiding in the bushes?" He scanned the area beyond the firelight.

Manny shook his head. "Just us."

Winston stepped next to Manny and looked down at Hayden. "Rusty, get us a chopper. Mr. Carlysle needs to get to a hospital."

"Right, chief." Rusty keyed his shoulder radio. Winston saw that Manny was also bleeding. "And this one, too." Rusty nodded and began speaking into the radio.

Winston turned to his deputy. "And let me see those guns." Rusty offered the two pistols to Winston. The sheriff took them and individually flipped open the cylinders, examined the primers, smelled each weapon, and closed the cylinders. He held them up to the three suspects. "Two from this one. Three from this one. I see three wounds. Who wants to tell me what happened?"

Keith glanced at Hayden. Hayden glanced at Manny. Finally, Manny spoke. "Me and Hayden and Keith were talking. Suddenly, Machuque bursts in like a madman and starts shooting. I fired, but hit Hayden by accident. Machuque shot me. My gun fell next to Hayden. He grabbed it and shot Machuque before he could hurt anyone else."

Winston listened to Manny and leveled his harshest stare at him, accusing him, penetrating his defenses, looking to catch him off guard while he probed for truth. When he'd seen everything, he turned the piercing light on Hayden and finally on Keith. "Is that what happened, Keith?"

"Yes sir," the boy replied.

He looked down at his bleeding friend. "Hayden?"

"Best I can remember."

"All right," he paused. "Then tell me why Machuque would come into your camp and start shooting?"

Manny answered right back. "Look at his chest. Something got him. Must've made him crazy."

Keith got to his feet. "Yeah, we heard wolves a little while ago. Maybe it was one of them."

Winston vacillated between suspicion and disbelief. He walked over to Machuque and stared at the head jammed into the sand, soaking in a pool of blood. He rolled the body over with his foot and studied the chest wounds. "Wolves, huh. Never seen a wolf around here."

He looked at the men and scrutinized each one a second time. They stared back and didn't say a word. After several moments he said, "Could be, I guess. Coroner will say for sure."

He moved on, strolled over to Hayden and peered down at him. "What were you three doing out here in the first place?"

Before Hayden could reply, Winston suddenly spun and faced Keith standing next to him. "Son, I've been looking everywhere for you. Where were you yesterday?"

"I was helping my grandpa fix a boat. We were there all day. Ask him."

Winston didn't hesitate. "Tell me about that fetish I saw you holding at your sister's wake."

He intended to shock the boy and was pleased to see that the question made him pause.

He watched Keith concentrate and then heard a relieved sigh. "It was Tito's. I gave it back when I saw him at the jail."

"Where'd you get it?"

"I found it over there." He pointed to the scrub in the direction of the canyon.

Winston felt he was finally making progress. "How'd you happen to find it?"

The boy looked at him with the most earnest expression he'd ever seen.

"Suzanne and I like coming here early. I rode out the other morning at daybreak. She was sitting over there looking out at the canyon. She was holding a tube, like a toothpaste tube, in one hand. I walked up behind her and when she turned around I saw her face was bruised."

"She say how she got the bruise?" Winston asked.

"No, she wouldn't tell me. I tried but she ignored me. Just unscrewed the cap from the tube, squeezed some red crème on her fingers, and rubbed it over the bruise. I was worried. I thought someone hurt her and it would happen again. She said to stop telling her what to do."

"She was with Tito," Winston said.

"Yeah, he told me later."

"Tito told me she was okay when he left," Winston said. "He didn't say he'd hit her."

"He told me," Keith said.

"Suzanne didn't know he beat up a girl in Jémez Springs?" Winston asked.

"No," said Keith. "I couldn't believe she was that naive. I thought everybody knew about that.

"Anyway, next thing I knew she was skipping through the sagebrush like a little kid. I sat down right where I was. I could hear her dancing around and after a while, I shouted at her, that she was being wacky."

"You suppose it had to do with Tito?" the sheriff asked.

"Now I do, yeah. But I didn't know then. She was dancing and singing a stupid tune in an awful high voice. I remember seeing the wolf icon and I picked it up. Finally I hollered at her to quit screwing around. All she said was, 'Okay, hero. Whatever you say.'"

"She was a cocky one," Manny said. Winston glared at him to shut up.

"I just sat there," Keith went on. "Then she got quiet. I heard her call my name, but I ignored it. Then she shouted that she needed help. I told her she didn't seem to want help. And that's when she shouted that she had fallen and was stuck.

"I jumped up, but I couldn't see her. I yelled. She yelled from near the rim and I ran over, but still couldn't see her. She yelled again and I found her stuck in a crevice under some brush. I almost fell into it myself.

"She was hanging with both hands from a tree root. Twisting her body and kicking her legs trying to get up, but she couldn't. She saw me and I told her to hang on. The crevice was narrow at the top and I had to wedge myself in, but I still couldn't reach her. I tried hanging upside down with my legs over one of the roots, and almost touched her."

The three men now stared at Keith in astonishment.

"She told me to stay like that and then she let go of the root with one hand and reached up for mine. I stretched as far as I could. My legs were losing their grip. She pulled with one arm, swung her feet and caught my hand.

"I grabbed her wrist and then she let go of the root and grabbed my other wrist. Her full weight was too much. My legs cramped. I knew I couldn't hold us. We were going to die. My legs started slipping. She felt it too. She was as scared as me. Then, my legs gave out and we fell. I'm not sure how I did it, but I let go and grabbed a tree root with my left hand. I must have somersaulted past it, but I held on and we stopped. I had the root like this," he held his left arm straight over his head, "and she was hanging with both hands like this," he dangled his right arm down from his side.

"I just screamed and tried to hold on. I knew we were going down. My arms were getting yanked out of my body. I knew I was going to have to let go. She screamed at me. I looked down and saw her blinking. Her eyes had dirt and tears. She looked at me, said, 'I love you, Keith' and she let go."

Winston regarded the boy standing before him and the tears running down his face. "She let go to save you."

"I couldn't believe she did it," Keith sobbed. "I just hung there and watched her fall. The way she bounced I knew she was killed. I was pathetic. I failed the most important person in my life."

"Sounds to me like you did the best you could," Winston said.

Keith sniffed and drew one sleeve across his eyes and nose. "Anyway, I got myself out of there and just ran. I think I ran all the way home."

"That's an awesome burden to carry," Manny said.

Keith clenched his fists. "I was mad and scared and crying. If only I'd listened when she first called me. I didn't know she needed help. I could have saved her."

Winston looked at Hayden, saw the tears on his cheeks, and knew they were not for his own pain but for his son's.

～

Rachael sat on the couch with her young friend, Sheila, and picked with her fingernails at the blue and green tufts in the cushions. She didn't like visiting Sheila's home because its dim lighting, ratty furniture, and burnt-cooking-oil smell reminded her of the lonely years she'd suffered by herself before she met Manny.

The two-beat Mexican polka blaring from the tiny radio in the kitchen drowned most of Sheila's words into the telephone. Rachael watched her hang up and turn with an ashen face. She felt her insides go loose.

"That was Rosa at the hospital," her friend said. "She said there was a fight. Manny and that scientist, Carlysle, were wounded."

She felt her eyes widen, her jaw drop. She couldn't speak. She saw the pity in Sheila's eyes.

"Honey, there's more. Terrible news." Sheila paused. "Sanrio was killed."

Everything inside her broke apart. She dropped her face into her hands, saw the shards of her life slam to the floor and scatter across the dark tiles. She rocked back and forth and groaned.

The more she thought about her predicament, the worse she felt. Finally, her woe turned to distress. She thought of Manny and how he knew, now, that Sanrio had wanted him dead and how she must have known about it. She began to wail in fear. "Oh, my husband."

She felt Sheila give her a hug, but it didn't help. Her body shook with every sob.

Monday

~

Hayden had healed well in the hospital and was released on Sunday. He spent much of his down time agonizing over his mistakes. *How could I let myself be deceived? I misheard Tito. I assumed a connection with the girl in Jémez. Worse, I didn't analyze the satellite video. It's as if I'd forgotten everything I knew.*

The day after arriving home, he managed to stiffly walk into Parker's office. Groggy and uncomfortable from his pain pills, he felt very much like an old man. The first thing he saw was the gyrfalcon. The bird spotted him and blinked. Then it screeched and moved its talons restlessly back and forth on the perch.

Parker stood to greet him. "Merlin's anxious, Hayden. Doesn't know what to expect."

They shook hands. Hayden looked at the chairs and remembered how difficult it was to sit. He opted to lean against one of the credenzas, but found that he still had to hold himself unnaturally erect to minimize the discomfort of the bandages under his clothes. He looked at Parker who stood by the bird and answered the implied question, "Not sure what I expect."

Parker gave him a look he could not read, "You know that the Army began its offensive without us."

"So we weren't that important after all."

"On the contrary, General Tolen wants the program delivered ASAP. Major Gray gave it a sterling recommendation."

"Does that mean they will accept our strict ethical position?"

"I don't know. Do you think they should?"

"Yes. Stronger than ever."

"You're flip-flopping again."

"A virtuous decision requires accurate intelligence. I learned that is not always present, and even when it is, there's no guarantee that human emotion won't screw up the outcome."

"Emotion overpowering reason?"

"Something like that," Hayden pushed the blood-spattered pickup image from his mind. Then he added, "Weakness of the human heart. Machines will do better."

"Major Grey won't be pleased that you're leaving."

"He'll understand. We've talked. He knows that I can't be the judge of life and death. Not anymore."

Parker regarded Hayden with a melancholy expression and extended his hand in farewell. Hayden took Parker's hand and saw the gyrfalcon eye him with a glacial stare.

~

That evening, Hayden stood on the rim of Frijoles Canyon with Lucy and Keith, not far from where he had been shot. The sun, about to set over the Jémez Mountains, lit the mesa in a warm rosy hue and hid the gorge before them in deep black shadow. They stood together, wearing Sunday clothes and holding flowers.

When the sun touched the horizon, the family threw their flowered tributes over the cliff into the darkness. Lucy wept and Hayden took her hand. She leaned her head on his arm. "Keith told me how much it meant that you went to save him."

Hayden squinted into the setting sun. Lucy waited for him to speak. Finally, he said, "I never told anyone. But when I climbed to save Suzanne—" He choked, his throat filled with moisture. "She was in my hand for a moment." He glanced at his wife and son. "Just for a second. Then I watched her fall. From my fingertips. I had her and she was gone." He clamped his eyes shut.

Lucy hugged him. Keith embraced them both. "We both had her, Dad. We both tried."

Hayden opened his eyes and looked into his son's face with a comforting smile. "I know, son. I'm so proud of everything you did."

~

Manny steered the overloaded Chevy pickup onto the shoulder by Grovenor's Stage Line and skidded to a stop in the gravel. Dust swirled around the vehicle and began to settle on the women's clothing and possessions thrown into the truck bed. Manny stepped out of the cab, turned unsteadily, and slammed the door. He cut a weaving, limping path to the tailgate, lowered it, and heaved the contents piece by piece onto the shoulder. The breeze fluffed the clothes, lifted some and tumbled them along the shoulder, scattered them in the sagebrush. Manny looked up and watched pieces of his wife's wardrobe catch on a new sign. It read: "Going Out of Business."

When the truck was empty, Manny stood by the opened driver's door, pulled a pint bottle of whiskey from his jacket, chugged a long mouthful, and clambered into the cab. He started the engine. The Chevy lurched forward on the shoulder. The tires threw gravel and it roared down the highway.

Manny's red eyes stared out of the windshield and he tried to focus on the highway that stuttered in his vision. The pavement wove back and forth and suddenly a wolf appeared in the headlights standing foursquare in his path. On reflex, he yanked the wheel to the right. He missed the wolf and watched himself sail off the shoulder, down a steep embankment. He felt the truck slam to a standstill. He was rolling and then it banged, teetered over, and stopped. He heard the wheels spin. Smelled dust whirling through the cab. He knew he was upside down, laying on the interior of the roof. He tasted blood and, for a few brief moments, stared at the cracks in the broken driver's window before they faded slowly to black.

~

Winston stopped the cruiser in front of the Carlysle Home and turned off the engine. *No Audi in the driveway. They must still be out.* He leaned against the car to await their return and listened to the breeze and the traffic rolling in the distance. The evening was still warm. Although he was relaxed he knew the discomfort in his gut came from yet another duty that meant unhappiness for his friends.

He watched the Audi turn into the driveway, its three occupants staring at him with that mixture of suspicion and concern that comes with the uniform. He pushed himself off of the cruiser's trunk and prepared to meet the family.

Lucy stepped out of the driver's side and looked at him with flat eyes and lips like a pencil line. She walked slowly toward him and stopped a few feet away. Hayden and Keith came around from the passenger side. Their looks questioning him as they came beside Lucy.

Lucy turned at Hayden. "Hayden, I asked Tom to come."

Winston watched Hayden glance back and forth between him and his wife.

"What's up?" he asked.

"I'm gonna take you downtown, Hayden." It didn't sound as neutral as Winston had intended.

Hayden seemed genuinely surprised. "What? Why?"

Lucy took Hayden's arm. "Hayden, please don't be angry with me."

Hayden turned to his wife. "What do you mean? What's going on?"

She implored him. "I know Manny forgave you for Tito. But I can't. I'm sorry."

Hayden's face darkened slowly. "Tito. Oh, Christ. "

"I couldn't live with myself if I didn't say something," she reasoned. "And there's Keith. It's wrong for him, too."

"Lucy, you are serious?" Hayden asked.

"She is serious, Hayden," Winston said.

Lucy turned to the sheriff. "Thank you, Tom." Then she looked again at her husband. "But I am so very sorry for you, for all of us, that it had to come to this."

Keith didn't like it. "Mom? Dad?" he said.

"Sorry, Keith," Winston broke in. "I know you've been through an awful lot over the last few days and this doesn't make it any better. But we have to respect the law." He turned to Hayden, "Hayden. Please say goodbye."

Hayden stood still as if deciding what to do next. He turned and embraced Keith. Winston saw tears run down their faces.

"It'll be all right, son. Go with your mom now. She's doing the right thing. I'll see you. Don't worry." Hayden let go of his son. Keith and Lucy backed away and regarded him from the driveway in front of their darkened home.

Winston took Hayden's arm and led him to the cruiser, to the side facing his home. He opened the rear door. Hayden stood, but didn't get inside. They studied each other for a moment, eye to eye, before Winston said, "I never would have thought, Hayden. What happened?"

Hayden looked away. "It took over my mind. I close my eyes. I see her face falling away from me down the cliff. Then, I just—" He snapped his fingers.

Winston regarded him with a grave expression. "We all have the capacity for anger and violence. When violence becomes lethal, life and death lose their meaning. I didn't think you'd get trapped in that cycle, Hayden. I'm truly sorry."

Hayden stood in profile, but Winston saw that he understood. "How did you fool the keystroke log on your computer?"

Hayden turned toward the opened car door. He looked tired. "Sorry, Tom. I don't really feel like talking."

"I can understand that."

Hayden lowered himself into the back seat and turned for a last look at his home and family. Winston closed the rear door and his body momentarily blocked Hayden's view. When the sheriff stepped aside, Hayden was sure he saw a large grey wolf standing by his home.

Winston's door slammed. The engine started. The car moved. Lucy and Keith waved. Hayden couldn't take his eyes from the wolf until they were out of sight.

Acknowledgements

Some of the discussions of automated weapons systems came from:

The Principle of Humanity in Conflict, **by Mark Gubrund, International Committee for Robot Arms Control, November 19, 2012.**

Governing Lethal Behavior: Embedding Ethics in a Hybrid Deliberative/Reactive Robot Architecture, **by Ronald C. Arkin, Mobile Robot Laboratory, College of Computing, Georgia Institute of Technology, Technical Report GIT-GVU-07-11.**

Hanna K. Jones improved this story's focus and continuity with talented editing. I am grateful for her caring and insightful criticism. Any mistakes or inaccuracies in the text are mine alone.